The Wardrobe Department

The Wardrobe Department

Elaine Garvey

CANONGATE

First published in Great Britain in 2025
by Canongate Books Ltd, 14 High Street, Edinburgh EH1 1TE

canongate.co.uk

1

British Library Cataloguing-in-Publication Data
A catalogue record for this book is available on
request from the British Library

ISBN 978 1 80530 236 0
Export ISBN 978 1 83726 019 5

Typeset in Bembo MT Pro by
Palimpsest Book Production Ltd, Falkirk, Stirlingshire

Printed and bound by CPI Group (UK) Ltd, Croydon CR0 4YY

MIX
Paper | Supporting
responsible forestry
FSC
www.fsc.org   FSC® C171272

Moling: Glúais alle go ttormalla
                cuid bhus milis lat.

Suibhne: Dá fhestá-sa, a chléirecháin,
                doilghe bheith gan bhrat.

from *Buile Suibhne*,
J.G. O'Keeffe (ed.), 1913

Moling: Come closer. Come here and share
                whatever morsels you would like.

Sweeney: There are worse things, priest, than hunger.
                Imagine living without a cloak.

from *Sweeney Astray*,
Seamus Heaney, trans.
of *Buile Suibhne*, 1983

London

Thursday, 28 March 2002, 11.15 a.m.

I got out at Green Park and started walking. What a relief it was to be above ground. If I went in the direction of Piccadilly Circus, turned left onto Sackville Street and cut through Soho, I would get fifteen minutes of open air between the Tube station and the theatre.

From the Ritz Hotel to the edge of Regent Street, I passed four famous buildings I had never entered. Double the number of houses I had been invited to in this country. Two homes in twelve months. An actor's flat, for an after-show party, and a semi-detached in Surbiton to meet my father's cousin and his wife. Not my idea. It had taken me three hours to get there, only to have them bombard me with their 'Why don't you—?' and 'You should—' instructions for my life. This is what had driven me out of Ireland, the 'Why aren't you more like me?' bastards. The pair of them bristled when I said my current landlords were Muslim and we got on famously, much better than I had with their Dublin counterparts. I didn't invite them to come and meet Mr and Mrs Hanif. In point of fact, had I invited anyone back to Kingsbury? No, I had not.

The pace on Brewer Street was better, slow-moving

taxis and stationary delivery vans. A mother and a young child in school uniform were coming towards me on the narrow footpath. Same eyes, same colour hair. Holding hands. When I started school, my mother had to trick me with the promise of sweets or a visit to the field with the horse. If she mentioned where we were really going, I'd get sudden pains in my stomach. Freezing on the spot when I saw the black railings, the open doorway. I stepped off the path and stopped to let the pair of them pass together. A magpie was perched on a sandwich board a short distance away. Eyeballing me, as bold as a leopard. I wanted to feed it my loneliness. Let the hungry bird eat it up.

I didn't stop again until I reached the opposite side of the street to the St Leonard Theatre and waited for a break in the traffic. Daylight was cruel to the place. Without darkness as a backdrop, there was no glow from the neon sign, no chasing lights over the canopy, nothing to distract attention from the hardened chewing-gum and cigarette butts on the granite steps. Uncle Vanya and his roses looked anaemic on the posters. Behind the glass doors, the paintwork was dull and grubby, waiting for the softer light of the chandeliers. Seven-hundred-and-ninety-four pairs of shoes crossing the red carpet made it glorious by night and threadbare by morning. Anya's clean vacuum lines that masked the stains in the public foyer were being walked over by the venue staff. She would have completed the actors' sinks and showers as I greeted Mr Henderson at Stage Door, signed for the dressingroom keys and clocked in for the first half of a split shift. Cooped up for the next four hours. Bypassing the scene dock, the shared kitchen, the Green Room with its mismatched furniture from past productions, some of it missing a limb, some of it peeling apart after months of abuse, I climbed the back stairs to Wardrobe, right at the top, where the temperature rivalled a tropical greenhouse. The skylight was sealed shut for fear of pigeons coming in to shit on us.

Within an hour, I had snapped a sewing-machine needle on the teeth of a zip, marked a trouser seat with lubricant and found one of Vanya's off-white shirts had been ripped to ribbons in last night's wash. Drop everything. Leave the place and don't come back. The impulse lasted as long as a soap bubble. I was not that brave. To get over myself, I propped open the fire-escape exit to the outdoor stairwell and took an early tea break.

Out on the steel platform, five stories high, the wind was as strong as an onshore breeze. My gut wanted to tip over the railing and return to the ground below, so I closed my eyes and concentrated on the tulip-shaped mug I was holding. Heat against my palms did the trick. I raised my face to the sun and thought about being at home, by the ocean. The gulls I heard were not ripping open bin bags, they were fishing in the channel, and wild primroses were growing along the side of the road. Anya would be back in the foyer, dipping a cloth in Brasso for the door plates, close to finishing up. As I brought the mug to my lips, I smelled urine on my fingers. From the pinstripe trousers. Replacing zips on tailored trousers was the most time-stealing, cursed job there was. Did I not want to cry about having to touch other people's dirty clothes? Unpicking the hidden layers and mashing them back together? Not so long ago, that is what I would have done, but after surviving three months of split shifts at the St Leonard, I wanted to drink the tea while it was hot. Lowering my grip on the mug, I stayed put. No one had forced me to take this job. The Breton stripes I wore yesterday. What was it Margaret said? 'Vertical stripes for the bourgeoise, horizontals for the proles.' Get the washing finished. Keep going with the repairs. The bottom rib of a finely woven cardigan with embroidered panels was torn at the back. A perfect 1950s replica. Snagged on a door handle when Yelena wrestled Vanya for the gun. Snagged again on a fake diamond ring when taking it off at the end of the scene. It would need a magnifying glass and me sitting round-backed making tiny duplicate stitches, cursing it for being dark green and not bright blue, and Sonya Alexandrovna would ask Doctor Mikhail Astrov the same question tonight that she asked him every night: 'Why are you destroying yourself?' I don't know, Sonya, I don't know.

I opened my eyes and had a little stare at the building on the opposite side of the lane. A red-bricked jigsaw, capped in grey tiles with a window in the sloped roof and a faded Union Jack on an aerial. Names of some of the occupants were slotted into an intercom panel down at street level. Buzz the fourth floor for a publisher's office. Walls lined with bookshelves, back of heads sitting at desks. I often spied on them, hoping to witness something interesting: a bit of drama, a famous face. A woman walked around distributing A4 pages along with an assortment of envelopes.

There was an unopened voicemail squatting on my mobile-phone screen. Probably a message I didn't want to hear. My mother was the only person who left voice-mails, to remind me I had a mother and should call her more often. Why didn't I? When I told her I had a break between jobs last autumn, the next I heard was a voice-mail saying she was at Stansted Airport, waiting for me. I found her sitting in Arrivals. She hadn't eaten since the day before. We ordered horrible sandwiches in a horrible airport café and, when I was buying tickets for the train, I realised she had left her luggage behind. Said it was not her fault, she thought I had it. It was either confiscated or stolen, we never found out. Had she not heard of 9/11? I spat with rage. She shrugged. Why was I being like that? I did not allow her to lay a hand on me for three days and moved away whenever she came close.

'You don't want me here,' she said.

I couldn't say 'yes' and I couldn't say 'no'.

There was a backdraft behind me as the door down the corridor slammed and hard soles secured with tiny nails tapped against the lino, followed by a heavier tread with keys jangling against a pelvis.

'Anyway, whose father didn't?'

In the room already.

'It's the same one as usual, acting up again.' Margaret. Waiting for Lloyd, the theatre's caretaker, to catch his breath. He was holding a toolbox in one hand and began patting the top of an ancient washing machine with the other.

'Sturdy old girl. Survived longer than my marriage, she has.' He sucked air through his teeth. 'Could be the bearings, or the belt, or the agitator maybe. We've prob-ably replaced almost every part of her bit by bit, but she's still going strong.'

I kicked away the stage weight propping open the

fire-escape door, wanting it to slam because I was annoyed, instead of self-closing quietly as I stood in a teapot pose, one hand on hip, expecting a bang that did not come. Margaret was watching my dumb show. I put down the mug and spoke too loudly.

'Except she isn't. She chewed a shirt this morning, shredded the sleeve to bits.'

Two days in a row. Astrov's socks yesterday. Vanya's shirt today. I went to the work table and held up the evidence that would send me rooting through the spares to find a same-size, same-style replacement, then make it lived-in, as though it belonged to someone. A character sinking into despair needed frayed cuffs and collars. The second machine had finished another load of underwear and towels, but I hadn't emptied it yet. Or sorted the delicates: bullet bras, longline bras, slips and stockings. Garters and girdles needed to be spot cleaned. There were ladybird-red lipstick and greasy pomade marks on linen. A lace glove was missing. The unfinished ironing. I would see endless metal poppers and pearl buttons under my eyelids tonight. And Lloyd was kneeling slowly, inspecting the drum slowly, smiling at the monster, and not fixing it.

'Hello, Irish. Do I get a cuppa as well? Builder's brew.'

'Lloyd, can you work your magic on the washing machine without distracting everyone around you? You know I love you, darling, but Mairéad is my assistant, not yours.' Margaret's tone was measured, almost quiet, as she scanned the room for everything I had not completed. She picked up the ripped cardigan and ran a finger and thumb along the damaged edges, as if she were calculating the exact number of stitches needed to repair

8

it, and noted the trousers I had left rumpled at the sewing-machine. *Too slow,* her face said. So different from her other, perfect, girls. Some long-ago Verity. Or Clémence. Who had worked like the wind, the absolute darlings.

'Have you started on the gloves for Ms Parker?'

Yelena's travelling gloves. Repeatedly wrung out and stretched in anguish throughout her goodbye scene, before being grabbed and kissed by Vanya. It made me feel sorry for them. Margaret had decided it was cheaper to stop buying new when I could cut out replicas to match the original pair. Improvise to economise. I was not paid enough to cut gloves. Or to fail at cutting gloves. Could Ms Parker not cut her fingernails instead?

'Not yet. The machine needle broke on a sticky zip.' I looked at my hands and then over at the stainless-steel sink in the corner.

'On the trousers you've left gathering creases? You know what, why don't I work in here? I'll get the paperwork and be back in a tick.' She click-tapped out of the room. That was what came of skiving and getting caught daydreaming on the fire escape. At least she didn't bite my head off. Her bite was terrifying. Anyone caught smoking in or near a costume would know the worst of it.

'In a right mood today, aren't we?' Lloyd was facing the open doorway and the corridor beyond. It wasn't empty. Margaret's pace caused turbulence. 'You know why she's so uptight, don't you?' He turned to me and tipped an imaginary glass twice to his mouth, then turned back to the machine. Whatever brand of tobacco he used really stank. I took in his stained fingernails, his patchy stubble, and imagined who was the more likely alcoholic.

9

'How do you know?'

He leaned back on his haunches, toes curled under in his flexible working boots, and spoke to my reflection in the full-length mirror beside the door.

'Everybody talks. Everybody wants to talk.'

There were cards, pictures and publicity shots on a noticeboard beside the mirror. Things we had added to our temporary workplace to make it feel less like a temporary workplace. A large dress-rehearsal photograph of King Lear, alone on his throne, had been autographed by the actor: *To my Angels of Wardrobe, XXX Harry A.* Given as a parting gift to Margaret on the closing night, which she had regifted to me because I'd taken that job at short notice. I had secured the photo in place with a pin between the actor's eyes. Lloyd's eyes lit up when he saw it.

'Harry Adley. What a legend. The stories I've heard about him.'

I crossed the room and began to wash my hands at the kitchen sink. With my head down, lathering soap under running water, I hoped Lloyd would understand I was not in the mood to reminisce about Harry Adley. *King Lear* was the first production I'd worked on with Margaret; she had hired me to replace a dresser who had quit. Three and a half hours of Shakespeare. Within a week, I had made a tool belt for myself. Discreet, flat-to-the-body, multiple pockets for a pencil, tiny notebook with my track order, a torch, pins, grips, tape, shoelaces, breath mints, tweezers, small plasters, a selection of needles, beige and grey thread and miniature scissors, looped on a ribbon. I never went into his dressingroom without those scissors hanging from my neck.

Lloyd tapped his nose with a screwdriver handle and then pointed it at me. 'Did you know he got them to spray water on his face backstage, before he had to carry out the dead daughter at the end?'

I did know. I was 'them'. It was glycerine and water.

'. . . and the audience, all gasping and "Look how he's sweating! How much it's taken out of him!" Canny old bugger.'

'Lech.'

'What?'

'Canny old lecherous bastard. "One kiss, luvvie. One little kiss on the lips. Slip your tongue in. Go on. Give an old man his last stiffy."'

I turned off the tap and tottered towards Lloyd with my arms outstretched, tongue lolling. Margaret was standing in the doorway.

'I didn't know that,' she said.

'Didn't you?'

I thought she did. She came in with her show reports, meeting notes, laptop, calculator and sat down close to Lloyd, cleaning the lenses on her glasses as she spoke.

'They took his child from him. Illegitimate. When he was very young. Put it up for adoption. He never saw it.'

People say the sun rises, the sun sets. It doesn't. We orbit around it. I hung the pinstripe trousers on the rail beside the fire escape, picked up the mounted magnifying glass from the shelf above the industrial sewing-machine and set it down next to the cardigan on the work table. Changed my mind, pushed them aside and reached for the fabric shears, the magnet of pins and a bolt of stretchy black nylon. Making a start on the gloves. The bright yellow seam-ripper glided through the old pair, giving

11

me a perfect template. She was not asking me to create an original pattern; it was a simple task of tracing the sections onto new material. Then why was I sweating?

'No pins in the mouth,' Margaret said, 'and use a rotary cutter.'

No smiling. No words of encouragement. Just don't swallow a pin and require lung X-rays and potential surgery. It had happened once, to one dresser in her care, so Margaret was fixated on banning 'pins in the mouth' forever.

'Would it not be better to use the shears?' I asked, 'for the finger and thumb pieces?'

'Yes. If we had nothing else to do today.'

With a pointed stare, she directed my attention to the cutting mat that had been left flat on the floor beside the mannequin. I picked up the mat and the smallest cutter. There was no reasonable excuse for my fear of using a circular blade. I had a qualification in fashion production. By no means top of the class, but still qualified. The other people on the course had been factory workers who had been made redundant and were pressing finished garments while I was mangling a collar or swearing over notch marks that did not meet. I spent a lot of time staring out of that second-floor window, waiting for the instructor to come to the rescue. She never lost faith in me, no matter how often I had to rip something apart and start over. I wondered if she would like to know I thought of her when I heard Yelena's line to Sonya: 'You should trust people, otherwise life is impossible.' Nylon is cheap, I told myself. Press down hard and don't let it move.

Lloyd had removed the lid, the facia and the front

panel of the washing machine, leaving its private parts exposed. He took a mug from the draining board and shook the loose screws from his palm into it.

'Back in a jiffy. Have to spend a penny,' he said.

I had noticed they did not say the word 'toilet'.

'Off to have a cigarette more like.' Margaret smiled at him as he left. The smile faded as she leaned her forehead on her thumb and index finger, looking down at a hopeless budget. 'Told you I was a lush yet, has he?'

'No.'

'No?'

'He didn't—' The cutter slipped too far from the template edge. I lifted it off the cloth, repositioned my index finger over the head and redid the cut. I was twenty-seven. I should stop being afraid all of the time. 'He didn't tell me, he hinted at it.' To my surprise, I blushed deeply when I said this.

'Old gossip. He can't help himself.'

She wasn't angry? She wasn't angry and I hadn't betrayed Lloyd, and I was shocked, relieved and confused. I started to ask a question and thought better of it. Yet I had to know.

'Are you?' I said quietly, barely raising my face to look at her.

'Does not drinking on opening night mean I am?'

'No. Obviously not. Sorry.' It was a nosey question. I stared at the table to avoid her eyes.

'Well, I am, darling. But I'm sober now, as you can see.'

She continued dealing with the numbers, trying to make the figures line up. I had never met anyone like her. Returning to my task, I pulled back the first section of the template. It seemed all right, but gloves were fussy things. Time-stealers, if you let them get the better of you. Taking a deep breath and whispering "Sé do bheatha, a Mhuire. Your help would be welcome here, Mary', I kept going.

2.30 p.m.

Lloyd replaced the rubber seal in the washing machine and might have stayed to tell us in detail about the importance of maintaining an extensive collection of spare parts if Margaret hadn't stressed how busy he must be, how many other jobs were no doubt waiting on him. I put in a load of towels on a short cycle, in case the chewing continued. It didn't. We had her back.

Margaret opened her diary. 'Scott Gilbourne is coming in for a fitting in half an hour.'

Scottish Scott. Doctor Mikhail Astrov. My particular obsession. Philippa was his dresser. She said he didn't eat before a performance; he sat doing a jigsaw or a crossword puzzle. Ate half a sandwich between shows on a matinée day. Lived on cigarettes and sugared tea the rest of the time, and, according to Philippa, his good looks. He was very good-looking. I had trouble standing close to him because I would be overwhelmed by the nearness of his skin, his breath coming and going, the shape of his lips when he spoke, his eyelashes that I could see in the dark. I couldn't be in the room with Scott and Margaret. It would be me, staring like a sheep over a fence post, incapable of concentrating on anyone else, including myself. His family was well-to-do, so I heard. A man who was used to other people paying attention to him.

'Why are we doing a fitting three months in?' My panic was rolling into anger. I had spent the morning smelling and touching the bodily fluids of strangers, as though cleaning up after babies, and I was expected to say nothing, be a good little elf and go on ruining my back and my hands in their service. I hated the way we were told, not asked, and I hated being subordinate. It came from the top down, of course it did. Oliver Bowe. A man who employed the young daughters of his rich friends, the kind who had never been shouted at before, because he wanted them to be too shocked to do anything when he started yelling. 'Don't tell me. It's Bowe, isn't it?' I was defiant. 'Reminding us that he is the producer and if he wants to overrule the designer, in the middle of a run, then of course we will make it happen. Good things come to those who don't deserve them.'

Margaret had taken off her glasses and waited for me to stop talking. 'Mairéad, I'm doing Scott a favour. He's going to be the best man at his brother's wedding and thinks he's lost weight since January. I just need you to write down the measurements as we go. Can you do that?'

I wanted to eat, but not in front of her.

'Can you?' she repeated.

'Yes,' I said. How she loved to remind me of my place.

'I'm not saying this to frighten you,' she continued, 'but if Oliver hears you badmouthing him, he will fire you on the spot. I've seen him do it and I won't be able to protect you.'

'He can't do that, can he?'

16

'He can because he makes a lot of money for his company, and they would probably get him acquitted of murder, unless — and until — he stops making money. It costs nothing to lose you; dressers are interchangeable to them. However, it will cost me. If you want to do something constructive, get yourself a diary and start keeping notes. There might be a day when you'll need them.' She went back to her laptop.

I watched her reading for a moment and wondered, What if I do keep notes, Margaret, but what if they are about you? Instead of asking her this, I lied and said I was going to inspect the clothes rails on either side of the stage. Racing down to the Green-Room kitchen, I searched the amateur hiding places, the salad drawer in the fridge and the highest shelves in the cupboards, found a packet of chocolate digestives sitting in a mug, rapidly ate three of them, then drank a glass of flat ginger ale taken from an open bottle on the Props' shelf. The state of the kitchen. A smell of cabbage and sour milk. Thank Christ I did not live with actors.

3 p.m.

He had undressed to a blue shirt and boxer shorts before I managed to close the door.

'Wouldn't she like to do it?'

The accent was like a cat purring. Deeply self-assured. Margaret turned from him to me.

'Yes, good idea. You've watched me enough times, haven't you, Mairéad?'

I had not. Such bullshit. Why was she throwing me to this tiger? My gut contracted as she handed me the measuring tape.

'Relax your face, darling, and warm up your fingertips. Bring over a chair and we'll do the hat and upper-body measurements first.'

Scott Gilbourne raised his arms like a ballet dancer in second position. Clearly enjoying himself.

Margaret extended her open palm towards the wooden chair as I set it down next to him. 'Take a seat, Mr Gilbourne. You're too tall for her to reach around your head standing up.'

He brought his hands back to his sides and then placed them on his knees as he sat down. One step closer and reaching forward, I wobbled, distracted when he made direct eye contact, and almost toppled over with the urge to tilt his mouth to meet mine and kiss him. I flexed the tape sharply to rebalance, angry at him for staring, angry at myself for letting him. He gave me a half-smile. Bollocks. Expecting me to faint, or melt. I stuck a thumbnail into my palm as I called out the measurement.

'Head, 23¼ inches.' An undeniably big head. Good luck finding a standard topper to fit that.

'Why London? Why not stay in dear old Ireland, eh?'

'I wanted to be a director.' He had rattled me; I had not intended to say that in front of Margaret and glanced at her after I spoke. She must have suspected I had other ambitions, but her face was blank. I'd broken cover and no one was coming to help.

'Not many women directing theatre shows in Dublin, are there?'

He'd been to Dublin and nowhere else in Ireland, I assumed, if he thought I had a Dublin accent.

'I'm not from Dublin.' The sharpness in my voice was intended to silence him as I brought the tape around his neck and kept two fingers behind it. Slightest touch of his bristle. Softer chest hairs visible below. 'Collar, 15 inches,' I said. 'You can stand up, Mr Gilbourne.'

While he repositioned himself, I carried the chair to the work table and tucked it under as tightly as possible. When I turned around, he was facing forward, blatantly looking me up and down.

'Is it comfortable?' Margaret asked, 'what you're wearing?'

Squashed into a crew-neck T-shirt that made no

allowance for breasts and viscose trousers that bunched at the groin. I opened my mouth to say 'No.'

'Your shirt, are you happy with this one?' She was talking to him.

'This one is perfect,' he said.

His shirt was first-rate. Clean, tight stitching. Scent of washing powder. Carefully pressed. Nothing I owned fitted me properly, but this was not the place to admit how unhappy shopping made me and how I'd lie to myself about adjusting the thing, when I had the energy, in order to get out of a claustrophobic changing room. Day after day in the wrong outfit. Why were we not born with a coat of feathers? I used to delude myself with the notion that I didn't work in fashion, I worked in theatre. A forgiving space. Where people commented on my appearance frequently.

'Right. Then we can use it as a guide, Mairéad.' Margaret gave me an encouraging look.

I called out, 'Chest, 38½.'

If I wore better clothes, I would not be like this. What was the right outfit? Other dressers wore actual dresses. Jacqui often found lovely pieces 'for a quid' in charity shops. My arm would be too wide for their waistlines, never mind my hips. I couldn't wear a long skirt at work and I couldn't wear a short skirt on the Tube. Some bastard spying between my legs from the opposite side of the aisle, another one below me on the escalators.

'Let me guess. Maw is a dressmaker and you were stitching your own bonnets in the cradle?'

Why was he asking about my mother? To appraise me, as if I were stock. He wanted to open my mouth and check the condition of my teeth. It was none of his

21

business that my mother hadn't enough patience to teach. Tell him nothing. Get out of his eyeline. I tried to do the waist measurement from behind.

'You can tell where the navel is from there, can you, Mairéad?' Margaret had cocked her head, an eyebrow raised in amusement. There was nothing funny about surveillance. I held the tape between my finger and thumb and walked it around his torso, wanting to shout at them to stop watching, to leave me alone.

'Waist, 33¾,' is what I said instead, then retreated behind him again. Three-quarters of anything was not a measurement you'd get in a chain store. Standard sizes were the problem. I should stop buying mass-produced things, make all my clothes to measure and never get up from the sewing-machine. 'Length from the neck, 28.' The shape of his back was beautiful. I wound the tape around my palm as I pulled my hands away and told myself to hurry up and get the trouser measurements over and done with.

He placed his hands on my shoulders as my arms encircled the widest part of his backside. It was the lightest contact. Another dresser would barely have noticed it. Not me. A set of claws, a double row of pointed teeth, had hooked my flesh. The words 'one kiss, luvvie' tore through my nerves, causing me to shake my head in a sharp 'No'. I stepped back abruptly, palms facing out to push him away. I could not let him touch me.

'Sorry,' he said, with a little stumble forwards, a confused smile.

I was also confused. He was apologising. For making me feel uncomfortable?

'Cross your arms over your body, like this, please,' I said.

Rearranging my forearms like an effigy on a tomb, I made a show of demonstrating the next pose.

He did so and I averted my face as I went close to him, trying not to touch the fabric of his boxer shorts. 'Seat, 39.' He clenched and unclenched his fists. I had forgotten to take the arm length. How lavish was this wedding? 'Raise your arm as if you're looking at your watch, please.'

'Not Maw? Ah, your da is a tailor then, isn't he?'

'Sleeve, 34.'

There was a loud rumble from my stomach followed by a wave of pain in my bowels. My face turned puce as I clenched my pelvic floor and held my breath, sweating with the effort to contain the sensation.

'You are a shy one, aren't you? Got yourself a shrinking violet, Margaret? Well, well.'

'We all started somewhere, didn't we, darling? You're doing fine, Mairéad. What's next?'

The inside leg was next and I wanted to be sick into my hands.

'Shoe size?' I mumbled, not waiting for Margaret's reply.

Kneeling was out of the question. Squatting, however, was a bad decision.

'Am I right, is Da the one who inspired you to lift up the scissors and pins?'

It happened silently. I felt the stitches of my trouser seat loosen and separate along the seam. From stem to stern. As the stupid measuring tape dangled from my right hand, Margaret had a comprehensive view of my backside. Placing my left hand on my lower back, I tried to cover the gap between the elastic rim of my knickers and the cleft of my bum. I sensed her moving behind me. She didn't speak but I knew she had seen my mottled arse. Mortification made me run to the door and pull it back hard and fast, as if I were running for my life. His laughter started as I fled down the corridor.

In front of the mirror over the bathroom sink, I told myself I couldn't do this job, I'd have to leave, find something else. That would be easier than going back in there. What if it had repelled him, when he touched me? He probably rated the female staff on a sliding scale. From fuckable to unfuckable. I'd been trapped in enough all-male company to know whether I was valuable or not. Tears and snot slid down my face. I blew my nose repeatedly and it began to bleed. Fuckit all to hell. I stayed in there, dripping snot and blood, waiting for the shame to fade. No one outside of this building would sympathise. 'Arrah, pity about you,' my grandmother would say. 'Who will remember it when you're dead?' The need to go home, to hear someone with my own accent saying things I understood, hit me like grief.

'You came back. I thought you'd absconded.' Margaret had stayed in the room, the screen of the laptop reflected on her lenses.

'I was in the toilet.' Yes, I said *toilet*. What did it matter? Had I not just walked through the building with my underwear on display?

'Mr Gilbourne is gone. You can take off your trousers and run them up on the domestic.'

I put on one of the dressinggowns we kept for actors before standing in front of her, barelegged.

'Margaret, I apologise.' I was blushing again.

'Why did you run away?'

'Mortification.'

Her face tightened. 'Mairéad, we live and die by our reputations in this business and you need to learn to respond to the person you're fitting. They are in your care. You behaved like you were measuring him for the gallows.'

Shut up and take the correction, I told myself, and then retaliated immediately.

'He wouldn't stop asking personal questions. Why does he need to know what my parents do?' If a fella wants to know about the neighbour on his right, my dad would say, he'll ask the neighbour on his left. You did not share information, you concealed it. In case it was used against you.

'How often has someone asked you about you, without wanting something in exchange?' Margaret demanded. 'He was taking an interest. All he ever wants from me is scandal: Who else have I seen? Who's in? Who's out? Did I hear the latest? Conversation in this place is like practising fencing. One wrong word and you'll feel the tip of a blade at your throat. Bloody dangerous, most of the time. But sometimes it is not. Tell them your father is a tax inspector and your mother is a traffic warden, if you like, but then find something to talk about.'

I didn't know how to respond. Not talking was bad manners? The idea of my father becoming a tax inspector was laughable, but I let it sink in. Couldn't have come up with a better contrast for the man who had no bank account. Margaret's eyes were surveying the room. The replacement shirt I had found but hadn't broken down yet. Scott Gilbourne's vests, folded and stacked in a small rick on a stool in front of a tumble-dryer. His red Cuban shirt was laid out on the ironing board, another unfinished job, where I had been pressing the box pleat in the back. The pleat that stayed under a leather jacket for the entire scene. She fixed her gaze on me.

'Nobody should want to be in here for longer than is necessary. There are nine actors to attend to. Let's not use up all our energy on one of them, shall we? Besides, and I say this out of kindness, my darling, but he wouldn't battle rush-hour traffic for you.'

I looked up to the ceiling to contain myself and the full force of the fluorescent tubes brought on the need to sneeze. Which I did, raising my elbow to cover my face, and the image of his back and shoulders returned. She had found me out and I couldn't take any more attention. I was also annoyed with her. The politeness. The thin lips. Vigilant against displays of real feelings. Her lack of self-doubt. The waistlines of her skirts and trousers were smooth and flat next to her skin. Her seams would not burst open as she squatted to straighten a hem, to buckle a T-bar, to unplug a riding boot. Burst open. The embarrassment of undressing, of being undressed. Of how much our bodies needed love and how much fear we fed them. The truth was I had run because I was too close to his body when he touched my shoulder. Briefly. And it felt like being branded. My chest sank.

'Maybe I'm not cut out for Wardrobe,' I said. I was scared every day. I did not know what I was doing, what I would be asked to do next and when I'd have to admit I wasn't up to it. The split shifts were too difficult, I shouldn't have talked Margaret into letting me work so many hours.

She had already stitched some of the nylon glove parts together and held them up: the sections matched evenly, nothing amiss. 'I think you are,' she said. 'In fact, I think you might have a flair for cutting.'

That was news to me. Did she mean it, or did she say it because she didn't want to be left doing the work on her own? I brought my trousers over to the household sewing-machine and began unpicking the broken threads.

'I don't know anything about fencing,' I said. 'Wasn't much demand for it at my school.'

'Hockey school, was it?'

She was smiling and I felt grateful to her.

'Polo,' I said, relaxing enough to ask her something else. 'What were you talking about when you came in this morning, with Lloyd? You said: "Anyway, whose father didn't?"'

She appeared to be rewinding the day in her head, trying to remember.

'1952. Zsa Zsa Gabor in a Schiaparelli dress. Those leg-of-mutton sleeves. Lloyd told me about it. It's on in Russell Square. He likes old movies. Go and see it.'

'See what?'

'*Moulin Rouge.*'

'Did you go to the cinema with Lloyd?' I pursed my lips and dipped my chin at her.

'Yes,' she said, loosely shaking a finger. 'As friends. You can keep that to yourself, all right?'

As I made a sign of the cross over my heart and closed an imaginary zip on my mouth, I thought it was an opportunity to ask her for money.

'The notes from last night's show said the seamed

stockings are all ripped. Can I take some petty cash to buy more in Oxford Street on my break?'

'Old Compton Street is better.'

'For tights?'

'For sex shops. You'll get them cheaper there.'

My mouth ran dry. Margaret stood up and brushed her hands down the front of her skirt.

'Anything else?'

She was sending me to a sex shop, to walk through a doorway with a neon-pink 'Pervert' sign pointing down at me. Someone would find out. Someone would tell everyone at work and I would be ridiculed. Someone Irish would hear of it, and it would get back to my cousins at home and then my parents. I held the thought on my tongue a bit longer, swallowed it, replaced it with another: *What of it?*

'No. Nothing else. Thanks for the tip.'

3.45 p.m.

It was my own fault, arriving too early this morning because I was worried about getting clothes dry. The sleeve-eating washing machine had slowed things down, but I was left with the dilemma of time to kill before the evening shift and nothing urgent enough to keep me indoors any longer. Collars, cuffs and lace gloves all done. Vanya's burgundy V-neck almost dry in the hot box. There was maybe half an hour of ironing left and I could pick it up at 7 p.m., when I was being paid to do it. That wasn't true. I'd be back earlier than rostered, same as usual, checking hemlines and underwear, in a lather until each piece was set in its right place half an hour before the show.

My recurring numbers came out to harass me as I walked along Shaftesbury Avenue. Wages: £220 per week, give or take, after tax. Spent £28 on a 7-day travelcard. Put by £75 for rent, £25 for bills. Which left £92. Fine, no problem. Apart from the £85 I'd spent on ceramic fillings with Dr Paphak last month. Jesus, when the receptionist called out the total, I wanted to reverse the whole procedure, tell her to take them out. I had no idea it would cost so much – £85 on two blobs of porcelain. Deep breaths. There would forever be more sewing and more laundry calls to take. Put by a little bit each week for going back to college, before my rent goes up. I imagined spending daylight hours at the London College of Fashion. That would change things. Philippa was doing a postgrad and surviving. There was no reason I couldn't manage working and studying as well.

A sharp nip caught me in the stomach as I crossed the road into Soho. No pins in the mouth. But take them out of your clothes before you go walking. I moved the pin into the thick edging of my canvas bag. A baked potato at the Greek deli would have been nice. Or the old-fashioned café with the Formica table tops and white tiles on the walls, same as my grandmother's kitchen. Hot minestrone would be lovely. A pot of tea. A full plate of seafood risotto for £4.50. Choked on a fish bone in there before. Cut my oesophagus and couldn't swallow properly for three days. I was full, but kept eating the food I did not want with the twisted feeling that I couldn't waste it; the kitchen staff would judge me, it would rot in the bin. The same as throwing away good cloth. But, money. I had been making the same sandwiches for months. Supermarket cheddar, slices of dried figs and a green apple. What had I eaten yesterday evening – one kilo, two kilos? If I hadn't, would this morning have been different? I had read about gastric bypass surgery. You ended up with a stomach the size of a thumb and a wired jaw that was unwired once a week to brush the teeth. How would it smell, the tongue, the breath? Wired shut. Nutrient-deprived for life. Margaret ate things like a small bowl of string beans sprinkled with parmesan. Or a single biscuit and black tea. Or a hard-boiled egg with a dash of salt, followed by one filtered cigarette in her office.

There was an Anglican church nearby with a bench overlooking a pair of flat gravestones. I'd sit and let my feet crunch across the gravel, eating with my jacket on, in silence. When I got to the bench, however, I decided not to eat the sandwich. I could eat the apple and leave it at that for today. Exercise my willpower. A robin's song in the nearby trees sounded like bright coins dropping.

To stop myself from thinking about eating, I went back towards Charing Cross Road to browse the bookshops. Disappointingly, too many of them had that cover on display: the one with the woman standing in nothing but her floral knickers, with the name of the author and the title stamped across her chest. Same distressing feeling as seeing war photography. I could go to the National Gallery and stare at portraits of lacemakers and spectacularly hairless, naked women. The shock at seeing the darkness of underarm hair on a boyfriend at home, and then the sensation of moving my hand over his downy chest and stomach, not touching the skin, but letting the strands tickle my palm, came back to me when I saw those images. 'You like hairy?' he'd asked. What was wrong with hairy? Why wasn't *I* allowed to be hairy? He tried to touch me at the same time, but I'd trapped his fingers in mine and lifted them away. There was no pleasure in remembering. It was a curse, being unable to feel safe.

The Wallace Collection. That would keep me out of the shops. I walked through Soho once more and stopped at the sight of a bookshop upstairs, sex shop downstairs on Old Compton Street. Unbelievably, it had a

31

neon-pink arrow in the stairwell pointing to the 'Adult Section' below.

I had expected lots of man-made fibres and sweaty plastic vinyl. What I found was a bored assistant surrounded by glass display cases stocked with brightly coloured rubber dildos and sex organs that looked like jelly moulds. The pleated curtain running under the counter was red velvet, at least, but needed steaming and brushing. It was a disappointing toy shop. I bought all the seamed stockings they had, which were incredibly cheap, and left.

In a reverse of my morning self, I crossed Regent Street at the same spot and this time wandered up Savile Row, admiring the window displays and daydreaming about being apprenticed to a tailor. Crossed Oxford Street and kept going north until I found the Townhouse Museum on what seemed like its own island with expensive cars parked in a circle around it. A man in a blue suit greeted me at the entrance and handed me a leaflet with a floor plan. The excess. More was definitely more. Every surface was ornamented. The elaborate patterns on the wallpaper matched those of the curtains; the swags, tassels and tails on the curtains mirrored the costumes of the people in the paintings on the walls. Underpinned ladies with exposed décolletage wearing as much upholstery as a suite of furniture. The weight of their clothes. What would it do to your hands to have to create those outfits? The painting I recognised was the woman in meringues of pink and white silk, captured forever by Monsieur Fragonard, kicking off a dainty slipper from her cushioned swing, while a man lying in the middle of a rose bush, hat in hand, pointed at the gap between her many skirts. Philippa said they did not wear knickers.

They weren't invented, she told me, before it was discovered that women had legs. 'When was that?' I'd asked, not believing a word of it. 'Crinolines. When the massive hoops blew up and over women's heads, it knocked them face-down in the street. And there they were, a pair of legs, as shocking as a mermaid's tail.' I sat on a beautiful window seat and thought about who had suffered for this display of wealth.

5.45 p.m.

The smell of the theatre covered me as I returned through the stage-door entrance. Gunpowder, pine-scented cleaning fluid, old carpet, tobacco, leather, copper wire, burnt orange. It was too early to go back inside, but it would be getting dark soon.

'Evening, Mr Henderson.'

'Evening, Miss. Warm enough for ice cream, isn't it? Or a beer.' He was using an envelope as a fan, pointing it at me as he spoke. 'I have a block of raspberry ripple waiting at home.'

'You don't fool me that easily. We all know you'd much rather stay here with us and run around backstage in your blacks.'

He rose to the jibe and smiled. 'Might even get myself some cherries to put on top. Retire to the west wing and put my feet up, oh, round about 8 p.m.?'

My turn to smile, then to drop it instantly at the empty space behind him. 'No dry-cleaning delivery?'

'Caught up in rush hour, I expect. They've never failed us yet, have they?' His calmness was reassuring. The costumes would get here, whether I worried about them or not.

'Qué será, será, Mr H.'

'That's what my mama says.' He winked, tapped the envelope lightly on the counter and then turned around to the shelf with the logbooks.

I went upstairs and continued with the ironing. Lloyd came in and leaned against the draining board. Said he had come to check on the washing machine and to borrow a pair of scissors. I told him he could go down to Stage Management and use theirs. They would probably give him short shrift as well, but I didn't want to have to sharpen our best shears after he used them to cut cardboard or plastic or whatever botched job he was doing. He didn't go. Skiving or hiding from someone, I was sure of it, but I let him be and concentrated on getting a sharp crease down the centre of Maria Vasilievna's wide-leg trousers.

'You'll watch the World Cup this summer, won't you? Or are you too stuck-up for that?' Lloyd called me stuck-up because I bought 'posh' tea and didn't drink the dyed gravel from the Green-Room kitchen. He asked the question like he was throwing a ball, wanting me to join in, but it wasn't the right topic. My mum occasionally watched snooker or tennis, when they showed it on TV late in the evening, as a way of winding down. My dad preferred dogs and horses, for the opposite reason. Neither of them watched football.

'I might, Lloyd, for a while, but I won't feel a part of it. And I'm not completely stuck-up. I can admire their lovely kits.'

He didn't seem to hear this, possibly because I released an industrial burst of steam from the boiler. The tank refilling with water sounded like infected lungs.

'You never know, you have the two Keane lads – decent manager, the luck of the Irish, right?'

'Lloyd, I can't talk football.'

'No skin in the game, innit? It's all right, Irish, I get it. You're not sporty.'

Did he look at my waistline as he spoke? I set the iron upright and studied him for a moment. 'How many girls did you play matches with, growing up?' The question puzzled him. I kept talking. 'Imagine if you did. Imagine if one of them scored a goal against you and then their team won the league, or whatever it was, because of her. Would you think, "Oh, we should have girls on our team too"?'

'Mixed? That's different. You can't have—'

'I have a cousin – Brian – who said he could beat me and his sister by himself. First and only grandchild until he was five. Authority on everything. Olwen was twelve months older than me and I was the youngest. That was the pecking order. But Brian couldn't beat us, so he wrote his name all over the football and said we were not allowed to touch it. I'd say he took it to bed with him, to keep it safe from girls.'

'Brian sounds like a right laugh. Pity you didn't keep it up, eh? Become a striker?'

'I could have been a different person, Lloyd. Getting stuck in, fighting for possession. Brian runs a construction business in Boston.'

'But you wouldn't want to be sharing the boys' dressingrooms, believe me, Irish. Proper stink.' He pinched his nose and I was rolling my eyes when he said, 'Can I ask you something?'

'You can ask.'

'Do you mind me calling you that?'

'What, Irish?' The sailor collar on Sonya's dress wasn't flat enough. I pushed the foot pedal to boost the suction and draw the moisture out, but it felt like it was drawing more from my eyes and cheeks. Lloyd could not pronounce my name. Put him in a pub quiz and watch him list the World Cup teams from 1978 to 1998, but he couldn't manage to stress the second syllable of Mairéad.

'Doesn't keep me awake at night, Lloyd, if that's what you mean. It's better than calling me a Mick.'

'Let me guess . . . Mr Bowe, our glorious producer?' Lloyd released a grin that changed his entire face, showing his ridiculous gold tooth. It was very hard not to like him.

'Producers don't come up to Wardrobe, Lloyd, and dressers do not gossip. You know that.' I nosed the pointed steel tip of the hotplate into the shoulder seams while I tried to look serious. It didn't last and I cracked a smile to match the one he gave me. 'Go on, so, tell me why I should watch the World Cup.' I held the iron in a terrible impression of a microphone, the flex swaying from its hook overhead. 'Just the facts, guv'nor.'

His face changed again and he twisted away, examining the threads on the floor.

'When you've lived as long as I have, Irish, you think everyone will leave sooner or later, and they do. But not football. It's there, right where you left it, no matter what. There's a game you need to watch, a place you need to be and you can't let them down.'

'They're making a mockery of you, Lloyd. Taking your money and giving it to their greedy overlords.'

He lifted his head carefully, saltwater in his eyes. 'Don't you love nothing? Haven't you ever been blind about one thing and you know it's not perfect, it's not healthy? But you can't help it, being obsessed, because it's your life?'

This is what comes of talking without thinking. Or thinking only of myself. He was hurt and I regretted what I had said, but you can't unsay something. Once it's out, it's out.

'Cloth.'

It sounded stupid out loud, but I did not want to lie. There was no compulsion to hide from Lloyd. I selected Vanya's linen jacket from the rail. It was half-lined, striped viscose inside the body from the chest up, with a contrasting floral print under the collar. The sight of the two patterns together never failed to please me. I began with the buttonholes, smoothing my way out from there.

'How far would you get in one· day without it? When I pick it up, Lloyd, the feeling of what it could be. Touching fabric on display. Admiring rows of bolts stacked together. Colour. Weight. Texture. Drape. The way it moves when I work with it. The stitches I can use, the type of thread, darts, pleats, perfectly matched seams: making something that will be adored. If it's a natural fibre, it was grown in sunlight and fed and watered and here it is, between my fingers. What we need on our skin from our birthday to laying out our corpse – air, water, cloth.' Pausing for breath, I wondered why I couldn't say this to Margaret and Scott earlier, when they asked. I wanted to design costumes for the stage. Lloyd did not interrupt; he was waiting for me to go on. 'I'm sorry if I was being a prick about football. People think talking about clothes, loving clothes, is superficial. I happen to like the surface. We stroke the cat's fur, not the blood and guts underneath.' It sounded like I was seeking reassurance, but that wasn't what I needed. I needed to share some of the thoughts in my head with another human, one who wouldn't dismiss me, who would stay in my company no matter what I told him. I wanted to admit I had no one to hang out with on Sundays and I couldn't shake the feeling that most of the people here were concealing something, in case I tried to steal it from them.

There was some shifting of his feet, a raising and lowering of his chin, a short sigh before he spoke. 'She loved clothes. Adele. My ex-wife. Said she felt sorry for men because they couldn't wear skirts in summer.'

That was not what I had expected. Don't say anything, I told myself, just don't. His eyes were down, leaning back again, his fingers invisible but audibly drumming.

'She had this one dress, you know how it goes. Heart-stopping. Beautiful. I would have gone to war for her in that dress.'

I wanted to interrupt. What type of dress? What material? What colour? Belted? Zipped? High or low neckline? Was that the first time he saw her, or was it the first time he saw her as he wanted to see her? Was she less without it? A magic spell that lasted until midnight? What had happened between them? How much did he miss her in the morning and last thing at night? How much did he regret, and how lonely was he? None of these urgent questions left my mouth, for fear of silencing him.

'But Lord Almighty, waiting for her to get ready? You'd rig the *Cutty Sark* faster than get her in her glad rags.'

How should I have replied? I had no idea what he needed to hear. What did I know about being divorced?

'Maradona. More pigeon than matador these days, isn't he?' was the best I could come up with.

He throat-laughed once, sniffed and wiggled the tip of his nose with the back of his hand as he pushed himself away from the draining board.

'Diego Maradona. Yeah. Fat. And old. Well, I'd better shuffle off. Find a pair of scissors downstairs.'

He was patently dying to tell me something. Talking in circles, hiding out at the top of the building. These were tactics I used.

'I've never owned a dress like that,' I said. 'The kind you mean.'

'Haven't you, sweetheart? Why not? Clever one like you could make a pretty dress. Be no trouble.'

He was leaving me and my cleverness to finish the rest of the laundry alone and it stung me that I hadn't asked better questions. An angry stomach cramp hit me. I should have had a creamy seafood risotto, instead of running a time trial against myself between meals, hoping my clothes would be less cruel to me if I fasted. A lapse of concentration on the undersleeve jolted the iron too far forward and it caught the soft skin near my left elbow crease. A red welt appeared instantly. I swore and Lloyd turned back.

'I don't know how I managed that,' I said.

The burn mark mesmerised me. Lloyd was at my side and I had not noticed him crossing the room.

'Get it under the tap quick as you can, Irish. Give that to me.' He took the iron from my hand gently and I stumbled to the sink. 'I'll fetch Margaret,' he said.

41

Crouched over, eyes closed in relief as the cold water numbed the wound, I didn't hear Margaret coming in and banged my head off the shelf overhead when she spoke. 'Are you all right?'

Even though I kept looking into the sink, I could tell she was appraising the room and Lloyd had been sent packing.

'I won't be much longer. It's only a minor burn.'

Margaret stood beside me and tilted my arm with her strong fingers.

'Not that minor, darling. Did you put an ice pack on it?'

I hadn't thought of doing that, which I should have conceded, instead of lying about it. 'Couldn't open the freezer.'

Without another word, she unplugged the fridge, propped open the door with a large jar of pickles and started tapping on the compartment at the top, currently frozen over, until she found a weak spot and spliced it open.

'I'd be fantastic at cracking safes, wouldn't I? Let me wipe the ice off it first, then it's all yours. We really should defrost this more often, shouldn't we?'

We? I let the water run for another few seconds, then shook my arm over the basin as she scraped off the layer of fine crystals from the plastic pouch, wrapped it in a thin towel and placed it on the mark. Another scar to add to my collection. She was standing close enough for me to feel her exhale against my skin.

'Margaret, do you remember the first day of tech in the St Leonard? When I arrived stupidly early?'

Anya had been outside the front entrance, cleaning

the glass doors. Instead of admitting I had wildly over-estimated the time it would take to travel in, I told her it was my responsibility as a dresser to clear a space backstage for the clothes rails. 'Check with Margaret Gifford, if you don't believe me,' I'd said. Anya clearly did not believe me, but she let me in and watched me walk across the foyer, into a pitch-black auditorium. With one hand tracking along the wall for guidance, I inched my way down to the stage and climbed up. A reckless thing to do. And then to go fumbling around, believing I could find the light switches on my own. All I found was a cable to trip over and managed to ricochet off the corner of the prompt desk, pulling down an office chair as I crashed to the ground. I was on my knees, picking up the chair, when the working lights came on.

'Did you hurt yourself?' Anya called out to me from the stalls. I rolled the chair over and back on its castors to check it wasn't broken and then walked onto the stage to answer her. In front of me was a wide set of treads, wide enough for three people to step up from the audi-torium.

'No, I'm fine. I knocked over a chair, but it's okay, nothing broken.' The skin under my shoulder blade smarted a little. Surely, it wasn't? It was. Blood. There was blood moving down my spine and I was wearing a white shirt under a thin jacket. I threw off the jacket and strained my neck trying and failing to twist it far enough to catch sight of the middle of my back. 'Actually, do you know where I might find a plaster?'

When Anya didn't reply, I stopped turning in circles and looked out at the room. She was walking down the

43

aisle, a Front-of-House first-aid kit in one hand. We met halfway and sat side by side as I unbuttoned my shirt and pulled an arm out of one sleeve. Her cold hands rolled up my vest and unhooked my bra. She dabbed at the blood with a cleansing wipe and I had felt her also exhale against my skin as she pressed firmly on the cut to stop the flow. Then she smoothed a large plaster in place. Putting me back together in reverse order, she gave my arms a tight squeeze. 'There.'

The impression of her fingers and thumbs. I half-expected to have changed colour, like an octopus, with the flush of her contact.

'You've done that before, Anya, haven't you?'

'Three children. Two grandchildren.'

'Are you going about it the right way, do you think? Becoming a director?' Margaret was talking to the ice pack, bending my elbow to hold it in place. She did not seem to have heard my question.

'Is this about what I said to Scott Gilbourne?' I asked.

Her eyes were softly creased in either sadness or relief. She steered me into a chair and took the one beside it as I rested my arm on the table.

'Is that what you want? To be a director? Because I had wondered, you know, what you really wanted.'

'I did,' I said. 'I don't any more.'

'Mairéad, I remember that day. You were wearing a shirt that had been ripped and badly repaired, but then I noticed you had straightened out this room and were working your way through the notes.'

'I fell over, backstage.'

'I heard you went wandering around in the dark. Quite

44

unusual. That and the fact that you had read the play. Why didn't you tell me you wanted to direct?'

'I went to the Wallace Collection today,' I said. 'Doesn't it make you angry that the most selfish people are the ones in charge? No one would take me seriously, Margaret, not with my background.'

'I do,' she said.

This was my chance to tell her I wanted to study costume design. To ask for her help with the application. I took a breath, but she spoke first.

'It's comfortable, isn't it, the little cage you've made for yourself? And truly boring.' She turned her wrist to check her watch and then lifted the ice pack away from my skin. 'You need burn cream.'

Boring? She thought my life was boring? With decisive movements, Margaret went to the medicine shelf, took down the biscuit box with *Cuts and Burns* written in black marker on the lid and brought it over, standing with hands on hips as I opened it. Ointments, iodine, headache tablets, plasters and gauze were neatly ordered inside and the sight of them made me think of hospital needles and the intense pain of a hypodermic pushing into a vein.

'Start taking responsibility for your life, darling,' Margaret said as I applied the salve.

'It's not that bad. I'll soldier on,' I said, concentrating on not passing out.

'That's the spirit. Swords at the ready. Keep moving forward, with control. More haste, less speed, remember?'

I did not remember. What did that mean? The amount of things she said that I did not understand and was too shy to ask. The sound of her voice on the phone travelled down the corridor as I plugged the fridge back in and put the burn cream inside; the remedy was better when it was chilled. 'It was Anya,' I said to the leftover take-aways and ready meals. 'She is the one who showed me where the light switches were.'

6.30 p.m.

An internal phone call interrupted me as I was eating crackers, unhappily giving in to hunger, and I picked up the receiver on reflex.

'The dry-cleaning is here.' The company manager, Carol. Chief Luvvie Wrangler.

Thank Christ. 'Mh-hum. Tsks.' I tried to speak without moving my lips, but there was no disguising the lumps of carbohydrate mashed with saliva in my mouth.

'It's blocking the passageway at Stage Door. Could you come down and collect it, please?' Carol could co-ordinate a national emergency and simultaneously give a correct estimate of how much milk you had at home. She seemed to have a kinetic map in her head of what should be in place at the exact time it was meant to be. If anything was not running to schedule, Carol was there, calling out bullshit excuses.

'Yeh. Uh-huh. Sorry, Carol. Eating.'

'Yes, I can hear that.'

I let the food fall out of my mouth and into my hand, but she had hung up. The mush went into the bin. Carol would not be caught out speaking with her mouth full. Or saying 'toilet'.

Kilo upon kilo of costumes to carry up through the building. It made me resent Stage Management and their smug policy of employing men for their so-called 'heavy lifting' from the back of a truck to a dolly, from the wings to the stage, with maybe half a flight of steps to manage. Don't make me laugh. Try five stories – 112 steps from the basement dressingrooms to the top of the house. Try one shopping trip, one round of laundry. No one seemed to see this, not even as I went from dressingroom to dressingroom overloaded with their clean outfits. I put the dry-cleaning across my forearms to avoid straining my wrists on the wire hangers. The corridors were too narrow for a milkmaid's yoke, but that is what I would have preferred. A pole across my shoulders that could take your eye out. I started with dressingroom number one, hoping it was empty and I could do the drop-off without dealing with the temperaments of actors. When I got to the first floor, Scott Gilbourne appeared in front of me. My arms were pinned in place by the weight of the clothes; I might as well have had them tied behind my back as he paused, came in close and took my face in his hands. Was he going to say something? Was he running a scene? The food between my teeth. The smell of my breath. If he mentioned my trousers splitting open, I would have to leave the country. The hair and make-up artist appeared behind him, glancing, then moved on. Scott's eyes went to my lips and flickered on the tiny slits at the corners, the little cuts that appear like cold sores and stay and stay. Maybe the word 'herpes' came into his head. Maybe he was high.

'Have you heard anything?' Checking behind both his shoulders in a pantomime performance, he leaned in to confide. 'There's a lot of talk. About them making cuts.' His eyes moved over the costumes I was carrying.

'Do you mean to Wardrobe?' I whispered, wishing there was a seat nearby.

'Ah, I see. It's about the crew, isn't it?'

From each side of my jawline, I felt two fingertips trace the bone, meeting at my chin, which he held. To want. To want to shut the door of a dressingroom, to sit on his lap, to straddle him, pull him closer, never breaking eye contact, not speaking, moving inwards from soft to firm to hard. I tried to concentrate on the stocking stitch of his woollen jumper, but his smile was broad and warm.

'You've never been to a Scottish wedding, have you?' One of his eyebrows arched and I held my breath. 'We wear kilts, you know. My girlfriend loves it.'

He lifted his hands clear after he spoke. The weight on my forearms was making itself known to my lower back and I pushed outwards across my upper spine to relieve the pressure. A mobile phone rang behind a door and he checked for spectators again.

'Aye, well, better get to work. Don't tell anyone about the other. About the cuts.' He mouthed the word 'cuts' as he sidestepped away and left me standing, disturbed. Disturbed for hours afterwards. Margaret knew it before I did. I was ironing for him, hoping to come into his thoughts when he picked up a clean vest or a shirt. How often had she seen it? People like me predictably, so predictable it was boring, on a wild gander chase. I wanted to climb inside myself and stay out of sight.

A lemon swiss roll sat on the countertop in the Green-Room kitchen. There was a sticky note on the plate saying 'Eat me'. I draped the clothes over two chairs and cut one thick slice after another until I had gobbled the lot, to get it over with, before someone came in. It didn't help. I barely tasted it. A fucking kilt? Did his girlfriend know he went around embarrassing other women and touching their faces? I was about to drink a pint of water from the tap to flush out the food, but the water smelled of chemicals. The pipes were probably made of lead.

Philippa was sitting at the table, brushing her long hair, when I got back to Wardrobe. It wasn't lost on me that she arrived while I was out and then took the only chair with a padded seat. Without apology. Why shouldn't she take it? A degree in history and halfway through a post-grad in more history. She did not talk down her sewing skills or lack confidence in her ability to do her job.

'Scott Gilbourne told me they are going to start firing people,' I announced.

'Did he? And did he tell you the show is closing early because it's losing so much money?'

'Who told you that?' I asked.

'Nobody.' She went from brushing her hair to twisting it into a tight bun. 'But I'm sure it's going around. Stops people from thinking about their wages.'

The benefits of growing up in a house with a piano were not fully grasped by me before I met Philippa. Her family ran a business that was something to do with furniture; she said her mother was an expert on uphol-stery. They knew the theatre world and the art world and the fashion world because they supplied them.

'I spent most of today thinking about my wages.' If I couldn't work up the courage to ask Margaret, Philippa was my next option. I sat down at the table with her.

50

'What would you say if I told you I want to go back to college, to study costume design?'

Her hands stopped moving as she considered the question. 'Do you have a portfolio?' There was a small pile of bobby pins in front of her and she began securing her hair in place.

'I didn't study art.'

'Don't take this the wrong way,' she dipped her chin as she searched the back of her neck for fly-aways, 'but do you need to go back to college? Plenty of us, including me, including my mother, learn more on the job. I'm not trying to talk you out of it, if that's what you want, but it doesn't mean you'll get better wages.'

There were small oak leaves embroidered onto her blouse, black-on-black. You needed to pay close attention to see them. The girls in my primary school had been given pieces of gingham to learn how to use a needle and thread. We were supposed to use the straight lines of the red-and-white squares as a guide for backstitching and to embroider flowers using chain stitch. Our work was crooked and puckered, but I persevered.

'Do you regret it? Your postgrad?'

Any pins she hadn't used were scooped up and put back into her vanity case. 'I'm going to be the chief curator at a fashion museum.' She spread her hands as she spoke, unrolling an imaginary map. 'It's all part of the plan.'

'Another night of Uncle Vapid and Doctor Arrogant. I can't bear it. This show is killing me.'

The voice came from behind us, loud and bright. Jacqui. Spelled with a C–Q–U. Occasionally Jacqueline, not Jackie, never Jacks. Who told me at the end of our

51

first evening shift together: 'For twenty-one days in a row, hold a handstand for two minutes in the morning. It's a well-known cure for ageing.' She wasn't wearing a coat. Her only outer layer was a woolly hat with a pair of braids that ended in large pompoms dangling over her nipples.

'You two missed a fucking amazing party. Did I tell you about Lou, pre-show, yesterday?'

If I could have, I would have chosen to be Lou Hao's dresser because he had made me laugh at the technical rehearsals. On a coffee break, someone had asked where he was from and his reply was deadpan: 'The circus.' He had pointed one toe and swept a hand along his torso, 'You haven't lived until you've seen this body dismount from a trapeze.' Then he popped a whole macaron into his mouth.

'Walked in on him in his Y-fronts and he's blaring out "So Macho", dancing with the mirror, flexing his pecs and his cheeks – both sets.' Jacqui shook her pompoms at us and then stuck her bum out as she pouted. 'Thought I'd die laughing when he started twirling his moustache. I said, "Lou! Don't lose the socks. Here, look at me, I'm rolling them down for you." Every time, and I am not joking, every time he's getting ready, I hear this: "Where are my socks? You forgot the bloody socks, Miss Jacqui! Where are they?" What does he do with them?'

She dropped her massive tote bag on the table, left her hat next to it, went over to the cupboards under the sink and began taking out plates and cutlery, making a ferocious amount of noise.

'There was an actress, not here, who took the bedroom-scene lingerie with her at the end of the run, the set that had been the subject of three design meetings, four shopping trips, and of course she had no idea about any of that. I had to ask her to return it. It was very awkward. Maybe Lou is doing the same thing? Stockpiling socks? He could be. Enough to last him for the rest of his days. Did you get the seamed ones today, Mairéad? We're completely out. He kept on dancing, wanted me to join in, but I was too busy, I told him, too many people needing their socks rolled.'

Her voice carried over the kettle coming to the boil. I tried to watch for when she drew breath, but she was unstoppable. Returning to the table, she took items one at a time from her bag: her blacks, a make-up pouch, mints and various packages of food and drink. The taste of the swiss roll returned to my mouth and made me gag.

'And guess what? He took me to the party, for the TV thing he's in? I did tell you. I drank cider, God knows why, it gives me the shits, but I met the perfect leading man. Ravi. What a beauty. I am in lust! A flake, definitely.' She held a bottle of deodorant like a baton, pointing it at us for emphasis. 'Do not fall for actors; they always think they can do better than you. I only make exceptions for the most attractive ones. Remind me to go easy on the lipstick later. I intend to have some fun when I get out of here.'

I got up and made tea while the water was hot. *Did you travel all the way to London to be a skivvy?* my mother would want to know.

'Everyone in this building is so bland. Bores me rigid.' Jacqui dragged a chair out from the table and the noise made me turn in her direction, expecting her to sit down.

She remained standing. 'Do you think Lou will steal the underwear? He can keep it if it brings him that much pleasure. Are you hungry? I have stilton, water biscuits and that delicious orange-spiced chocolate that melts on the tongue.'

There was a brief pause as she stared at my feet.

'Mairéad, what are you wearing?'

'All right, Jacqui?'

'We've talked about this before. Hiking shoes?'

'You've talked about it. I like them. Waterproof.'

'I am telling you, for your own good, they are hideous.'

'I've been wearing the shoes all winter. Lou ran away from the circus.'

'Why are you telling me about Lou? You don't really believe he grew up in a circus, do you? Is Margaret here?'

'Yes. I don't know. Is everyone in here boring?'

Jacqui would laugh at me if I told her about the fitting with Scott and then the whole building would hear about it in sixty seconds or less.

'I won't get to see Ravi on TV and I'm livid, because I'm working every fucking night. I need to get out of this rut, I'm telling you, or I'll become a cliché. Honestly, Mairéad, you cannot wear them again.' She was pulling a face at my shoes. 'Donate those things to the army or a glue factory. Or burn them, I beg you.'

Instinctively, my fingers went to cover the fresh burn mark on my arm. Feeling the heat radiating from it made my eyes water. They would make too much fuss if I mentioned it. And they'd judge me.

'Get up early tomorrow and buy yourself better shoes. I'm not saying you need Anello and Davide. Just go to Selfridges. They don't stock clogs, so you should do well.'

'Cinderella,' I mumbled.

'Cinderella?' she repeated, turning up her hands with impatience. 'What about her?'

'Had to throw away her stupid shoes in order to run.'

Jacqui pulled her lips into a tight circle and her hands flew to her earlobes, squeezing them simultaneously with a finger and thumb. 'No, that's not what she was doing.' Her eyes were bright with the thought. 'That wasn't panic, it was strategy. Oldest trick. Leave something precious behind. Then he has to come looking for me. I might have to sacrifice an earring.' She fiddled with the clasps on the gold studs, opening and closing them with one hand, removing the right one completely to roll it around in her palm. 'Did you know there is a woman who arrives at the Ritz every evening for dinner at eight? In her gold tiara and real fur with its dead-animal paws, goes to the same booth and orders the exact same meal: steak tartare, frites and a glass of champagne.'

'The same thing, every day?' I asked.

Philippa shrugged. 'What's unusual about that?'

'Because, Philippa,' Jacqui leaned over the table, spreading her chest like a cobra, 'if you could dress in a tiara and fur every night, would you go out to eat raw meat topped with a raw egg and then go straight home?' She glared at us, mouth ajar, then sat down to cut a wedge off her block of cheese. 'Apparently, she doesn't touch the frites, just moves them around, and then sips at the champagne.' Tearing open the plastic sleeve, she picked up several water biscuits from the middle of the packet and put them on her cheese plate.

'I eat the same lunch every day.' I shouldn't have said that out loud. One more thing for them to talk about.

I bent down to put my head in the fridge, taking my time to get the milk and let the cold air draw the heat from my face.

'Because you don't live with your parents, Mairéad. And you didn't inherit a gold tiara.'

'How do you know? I might have the secret wardrobe of a princess back in Kingsbury.'

Jacqui snorted. 'I wouldn't put it past you. Clark Kent by day, Danny La Rue by night.'

'Lois Lane by day,' I said, pointing a teaspoon at her.

She raised a water biscuit at me. 'No, Clark Kent.'

'Piss off, Jacqui. I don't wear glasses.'

She snorted again and laughed out loud. 'But you don't deny being Danny La Rue, you massive queen?'

It was impossible not to laugh with her as I put three cups of tea on the table and sat down. Philippa spoke while reaching out for the cheese plate. 'How do you know about this woman, Jacqui?'

'My cousin Rollo worked there, in the bar.'

I put down the cup I was drinking from. 'You have a cousin called Rollo? That's his real name?' I was in no position to mock unfamiliar names, but you wouldn't get past the school gates with that one at home.

'Yes. Short for Roland. Why?' Jacqui gave me a particular look, the one where you believe they are going to pat you on the head, call you charming and romantic, meaning backward and superstitious, and go on to exclude you from the grown-ups' conversation. She chewed quietly, her eyes on me as she swallowed, before shaking the packet of biscuits to encourage us to eat, then dropped them.

'Last night,' Jacqui said, 'at the party, we were talking

about Bowe. His office staff have to sign NDAs. I imagine that's why Margaret is so protective of us.'

Abrupt. Impatient. Preoccupied. These were words I associated with Margaret. Protective?

'A gagging order?' Philippa paused with a knife in her hand and then sliced off another piece of cheese. 'That is appalling.'

At my brief introduction to Oliver Bowe after a preview, he had barked at me for using a mug instead of a wine glass: 'Drinking from pottery, I see. How Irish.' Didn't take me long to realise it. Here be a fucking monster.

Jacqui dusted off her hands. 'I can handle him. He likes me. And he could help me with my acting career.'

'Your *advertising* career,' Philippa said.

'It takes great skill to make pensions sexy. Producers recognise my talents.'

Jacqui's desire to be in his presence mystified me. 'Are you saying you're attracted to Bowe?' I asked. The idea of his body being close, let alone on top of me, pubic bone pounding mine, that voice in my ear, made me cross my legs and retch.

'Margaret must be. Otherwise, why would she keep working with him?' Jacqui said this calmly, as if it were a logical conclusion. I wondered if I had fallen down a rabbit hole.

'That can't be true. Anyhow, Margaret went to the cinema with Lloyd,' I said.

They both lunged at me.

'When?' Jacqui reached her arm out, as if to grab the answer.

'Who told you?' Philippa asked.

Our heads turned towards a pair of rubber soles and something metal marching down the corridor in a hurry.

'You have a fluorescent needs changing?'

Breathless from the stairs, a lighting technician filled the doorway. Combat trousers. Black T-shirt with some obscure band name. Carrying a portable steel ladder and a long cardboard box. What was he doing? Anyone could see there was no flickering light in the room.

'No,' I said, 'you're in the wrong place.'

'Yes,' Philippa interrupted. 'We do. In dressingroom five. I'll check if it's all right to go in.'

Another thing I wasn't aware of. I felt stupid for replying. Philippa pushed her chair back from the table. Too far back, I thought, as she left.

'Would you like a cup of tea, Clive?'

How did Jacqui know his name?

'No time for tea. When you're finished there, ladies, I have a jacket needs bigger sleeves.' He raised the folded ladder above his shoulder with one arm, admiring his own flexed bicep. 'Too small for the guns.' He smiled out at her.

'When you're finished with your tubes, young man, I have a kettle that needs rewiring to toast bread.' Smiling back at him, mouthing the word 'plonker'. Philippa was calling out to him from the other end of the corridor. 'You can go in,' she said. 'Come with me.' Clive followed her voice out of the room.

The carton of milk was sitting out. I got up and replaced it in the fridge, pausing for a second to consider climbing inside and pulling the door closed behind me. Instead, I took out the burn cream and put it in my pocket. It would be all right to take it home, just for one night, in case I couldn't sleep. There were dirty dishes in the sink. I rinsed them while trying to splash cold water over my elbow crease. Telling them about Lloyd and the cinema was wrong, but I couldn't understand how anyone would want to have sex with Oliver. Half an hour after a show, that was the longest I'd spent in his company, and then only because Carol had asked. 'As Company Manager,' she had put it, 'it is my duty to get the entire crew to the Reception Room post-show. At the request of our producer. For no more than ten minutes.'

The entire crew swore under their breath, but we went to an awkward meet-and-greet with an actor Oliver wanted to impress. A Tony-Award-winning somebody I had never heard of, who sent the rest of the building into a tizzy. He, the actor, had asked if he could come backstage to meet us. All of us. Oliver preceded him, patronising a female journalist: 'A picture of me? Oh, no, I'm not the photogenic one.' His latest assistant stood close to him as we had lined up for an inspection of the guard. As Oliver introduced the crew, the actor was gracious, incredibly handsome up close, and was either performing humility like a pro or he was, in fact, humble. I could see why you would want him in your production. I stood in the background as the bar staff offered platters of canapés and French wine to the dignitaries. Should have brushed my teeth, I thought, watching Oliver protect the celebrity from bores and introducing him to the good-looking women. He found out it was someone's birthday and shouted: 'A magnum of champagne, immediately!' Carol had stared at Oliver as he said it. If she had had a knife, I believe she would have thrown it at his chest and left him for dead.

'Are you done with us?' she asked him directly, from where she stood.

'What? With whom?' Oliver faced the source of the interruption. 'Oh, yes, you can fuck off,' turning his back on her as he replied.

'Did you notice Violet prompting him?' Carol had said to Philippa and me as we filed out.

'Who's Violet?' I whispered.

'His assistant,' Philippa replied. 'She had to tell Bowe who we were before he could introduce us.'

Carol's face had remained murderous. 'I've been doing this job for fifteen years. If we went on strike, then the bastard would learn my name.'

Because he had kept us far longer than the promised ten minutes, I had to abandon the washing that evening and run for the last Tube home. Heart thumping and anxious, because of Oliver Bowe. An earlier start the next day, because of Oliver Bowe. He didn't know my name and I didn't pay attention to the names of the women who were sent over from Oliver's office, because there seemed to be so many. Although Carol scared me, I wanted to have the same amount of mettle. To make sure no one made the mistake of thinking I was replaceable.

The stinging heat in my elbow crease returned as soon as I turned off the tap.

'Yoo-hoo! Earth to Mairéad? I said, you did a nice job on the rib.'

Twisting my head over my shoulder, I saw Jacqui examining the cardigan I had mended.

'Miles away,' I said, shaking my hands to dry them and turning around. 'It gave me backache, hunched over like an angry cat. Did you see the shirt I had to break down, after the washing machine chewed the sleeve?'

'I can understand it,' Jacqui continued. 'A country estate on the Scottish borders, a place in Holland Park, the reputation of Midas.' Still going on about Oliver. It occurred to me that she did not rush through her pre-show list. Confident in herself or in the security that someone else would cover the gaps. 'He can be dangerously convincing: "I see a great future for you, Jacqueline, if you stick with Bowe Productions. You're exactly what we need. Wouldn't you like to learn how to get what you want?"'

'Jacqui, he's a bully,' I replied, wanting her to change the subject.

'Is he, really?' She widened her eyes and placed one hand on her breastbone. 'Then we must send word to the Knights of the Round Table. They will surely come to our rescue.'

The sarcasm didn't bother me. On another day, I might have batted it away, but something invisible was pinching my skin and wouldn't let me shrug it off.

She continued talking. 'Have you noticed, after a weekend in Scotland, he wears corduroy? Red socks because he wants you to ask what school he went to, that's obvious.'

Striding over to the table, I sat opposite her and leaned forward to make my point. 'I've noticed he speaks French in front of me because he thinks I'm a bog woman who never passed a school exam. "Il y a . . . un . . . problème . . . avec cette femme."' Once, discreetly, he had pulled

Margaret aside after a meeting and assumed I couldn't understand a word he said.

'How do you suggest I get out of here, except through him?' Jacqui snapped. 'If he wanted to, he could introduce me to the biggest directors in London and New York. He has helped a lot of people up the ladder, you know.'

I didn't know.

'Feistiness. Backbone. Celerity. That's what he likes. Watch him sparring with the older actors, like Ron Cooper. He gets a thrill from a good fight,' she said.

'Ron sticks his two fingers up at Oliver behind his back. I've seen him do it. He doesn't like him.'

Jacqui held her face in a grimace, as though I had asked her to get me tickets to a sold-out show. 'None of us like him, Mairéad.'

Antonia Weld was a name I remembered. She had been his assistant when he came to watch the producer's run, typing on a laptop in the Green Room while she waited for him. Got headhunted by the Royal Opera, where everything that glitters is actual gold. I was hiding in the kitchen when I overheard Oliver tell her not to sit her fat arse on the ottoman and break it.

'Then it won't look good in your drawing-room, will it?' Antonia shot back. When I asked her why she wasn't upset, she placed her hand lightly on mine and leaned in: 'It's such a relief when he doesn't find you attractive. Confuses him completely.'

The pinching feeling increased and I began to feel queasy. Jacqui sat with her back straight in her flared short skirt and black top. It would be unfathomable to her that one morning a zip would close and the next morning it would not. Or to have hair that was not glossy and couldn't hold a sharp fringe. Her skin was scented with dewberry. Actors were obedient for her, eyes closed, trusting as children.

'Don't collaborate,' I told her. 'He would enjoy it too much.'

'Don't fall into that trap, Mairéad, believing the easiest thing. I honestly thought you were smarter. For instance, you don't mention that he is a notorious romantic.'

'Who is?' Philippa had returned.

'Bowe,' Jacqui said. 'We see the stunning bouquets he sends on press night and a first edition of some kind, if he really adores the actress, but we don't talk about it. I heard he watched Alison in *Jane Eyre* at least once a week for the entire run.'

Philippa huffed and reclaimed the padded chair. I shut my eyes for a second, making the decision to be more generous, less judgemental.

'Why, do you think, is Alison Parker in nearly every Bowe production?' I asked.

'Because he's lazy,' Philippa said, wiping crumbs from her space at the table.

'But, do you think he's in love with her, even though she's married?'

Philippa and Jacqui stared at me for a second and then laughed so loudly, I blushed and reluctantly joined in.

'How do you know about Margaret and Lloyd?' Philippa asked.

'You can't. I shouldn't have said that. Margaret told me, and she told me to keep it to myself.' If she found out I had betrayed her, Margaret could tell them I had split my trousers.

'I suppose you heard what your boyfriend has been saying?' Philippa was addressing me.

'I don't have—'

'Mr Gilbourne? He's telling everyone.'

I was red–faced again, this time because of a pain in my stomach. Of course he was telling everyone about the trousers.

'The lead in a period drama. With the BBC. He won't have to endure eight shows a week for much longer.' She took a paperback from her bag and placed it on the space she had cleared. I exhaled slowly with relief.

'You've lost him now, darling.' Jacqui teased me. 'Catapulted to stardom. Temptations everywhere.'

Not enjoying the joke, I tried to put an end to it. 'He is not my boyfriend.'

'Mairéad, I wish you would let go of being the Virgin Queen.' Jacqui was shaking her head at me. 'If you think you can live without getting dirty, you're wrong. Lust leaks out from between your legs, just like the rest of us. You'll make yourself sick trying to deny it.' She broke off a square of chocolate from the slab she had bought and stood over me. 'Put this on your tongue and let it melt. Let it make a fucking cesspool of your mouth. Come on, open up and do not bloody chew.'

'Fuck off, Jacqui,' I said softly, turning away from her.

She put the square in her own mouth and made a sucking sound, pressing her tongue against her palate. 'It's so good, how can you resist? Maybe you are a saint! Don't worry, I still love you.' She leaned down and kissed my cheek. 'All better.'

'I'm going downstairs to do my checks,' I said.

'Hold on.' Philippa sighed as she spoke. 'You might

want to wipe the chocolate and lipstick off your face, Mairéad.'

I touched my cheek, where Jacqui had left a sticky blob.

'Philippa! Spoilsport.' Jacqui threw an open bag of rolled cotton wool at her and the little balls went shooting upwards, like a plume, landing at random across the table. She opened her arms and regarded the mess, delighted with the result. 'See? Isn't spontaneity much more fun?'

There were islands of fabric between us, sharps of different lengths and tips, trimmings and fixings, now beaded with these fluffy white chicks fallen from a nest. My grandmother said finding chicks was a sign of good luck. I picked up a cotton ball and used it to clean my face. Home, my home, was a hundred years away. The thought of the open sky over the sea sent a line of pain from the back of my eyes to my throat and scored out a hollow in my chest. I could be outside, watching gulls and hooded crows gliding over the sand dunes, coasting on the breeze. Their feathers, when they swooped past my ears, would rustle like shot silk. I wanted my arms to unfurl into wings and the roof to roll away until we could see the sky and let the wind do all of the work.

The two beautiful faces in the room were waiting for me to speak. I was not at home, I was here. With open-minded people. I should have told them about Scott, about what had happened earlier, about being so home-sick it robbed sleep from me, about longing for food and then being afraid to eat. How I could no longer brush my teeth without crying, the bristles in my mouth, my open jaw in the mirror. But I didn't do any of that.

'Would you like to come to Kingsbury on Sunday? I could cook or make up a picnic?'

They glanced at each other.

'This Sunday? My mother is visiting,' Philippa said. 'Sorry, Mairéad.'

'I plan to be waking up beside Ravi on Sunday afternoon,' Jacqui declared.

The chill in the atmosphere was embarrassing. I brushed my thighs industriously and took a deep breath.

'Time for dinner at the Ritz,' I said, getting up and walking away from them. 'See you at the interval, when I'll be polishing my tiara.'

The obvious response I should have given to Jacqui's glorification of Oliver Bowe came to me later, when the moment had passed. Margaret was interested in what you wanted to do, Oliver in what you could do for him. There was only one god. Dangling money in front of Jacqui, money that didn't exist. When Oliver was told 'No', I pictured Rumpelstiltskin stamping his foot through the floor. You heard him before you saw him; in the backstage corridors, through the closed doors of a meeting, on the phone to Margaret, shouting her down. Him with, 'The fact is, Margaret, I have more to consider than just Wardrobe.' Holding all of the cards, all of the time. Telling it like it wasn't. I had no doubt he would use the knowledge that she was an alcoholic against her.

Pound-shop Napoleon, Lloyd called him. To VIP boozers or investors, Philippa said, you would swear Oliver was next in line to the throne, a singular genius. But he spoke to staff as to a lower caste. What had

Antonia done to annoy him? Brought up the subject of overtime for working fourteen days in a row, she told us, at her leaving do.

There had been a festival or a conference. Oliver got a fee for appearing at events she had organised; Antonia did not. Exploded like Krakatoa when she asked to be paid for her work: 'Are you deliberately trying to become unemployed?' Then the fat jokes started. And the rest. If an actor said they had backache, if sales were down, if sunshine kept people outdoors and away from the theatre, it was Antonia's fault.

Why was I making money for this man? Closing off one part of my brain and ignoring what didn't suit me? What didn't suit me was that Oliver made things happen. People were drawn to him. For reasons that were beyond me. I was here because I lived for the chance to escape entirely into someone else's story. To sit in a dark room and have different voices in my head, even if they were make-believe. To have time compressed and space expanded and be transformed when it finished. I was doing this job despite him.

The light backstage was blue. An underwater, nocturnal blue. In the near-darkness, apparitions appeared. An actor in a pale coat separated into the shape of an arm bent at the elbow or a shoulder turning, disembodied. A pair of eyes would surge up, like the head of an owl in the woods. Things could go wrong. Things did go wrong. Repeated actions happening at the same time and in the same order was one method of managing the fear. First, changing into my blacks: long-sleeved vest under a loose shirt, jeans, battered runners. Then I went around ticking

67

handwritten bullet points, my list of preset costume pieces that I never stopped worrying about, to the background of fire checks on walkie–talkies, vocal warm–ups and our choreographed routine with hair and make–up. At 7.20 p.m., the control room played The Ronettes' 'Be My Baby' for the sound check. The song blared in the auditorium and was filtered and flattened through the Tannoy in the corridors, dressingrooms, workrooms and prep areas: wherever someone was carrying out their specific tasks to make sure we went up on time. There was a hierarchy to observe. The bigger the name, the closer their dress-ingroom was to the stage. Unless they didn't like being alone. I dressed Sandra Long, Ron Cooper and Lydia Browne; Sonya, Professor Serebryakov and Maria Vasilievna. Sandra took thirty–five minutes to change from her chic ready–to–wear into a 1950s–style teenager in a worsted cardigan and chignon. She was such a pro, I really did believe she could manage a Russian country estate and all its occupants on her own. Ron was double-breasted suits and quilted robes. Much like what he wore every day, from what I could tell. Ron and Lydia looked out for each other. Ron was happy if Lydia was, and vice versa. Lydia was dressed in Katherine Hepburn trousers. She had that quality, confidently self–contained. The meas-ured time calls from Stage Management, five minutes ahead of real–world time, kept the momentum up and the stress levels down. As the call for the actors in the first scene ended with '. . . and Mr Gilbourne to the stage, please', my heart rate was a steady beat.

At the St Leonard, on *Uncle Vanya*, I loved being in the reversed–out world of heavy felt stapled to plywood flats. Subdued. Lapsing into daydreams between transitions. Philippa and Jacqui had the adrenalin–rush quick changes — rewind out of one outfit, fast-forward into another — while I stayed out of sight of the audience, sheltered by a cloak of blue-black.

Lou Hao, our loveless Telegin, brought me back to the present. After his last exit in the first half, he rushed over and grabbed my arms. 'They laughed,' he whispered. 'They've never laughed like that before!' I swear his grip was tighter, his face much closer than it would have been if we were in daylight. He lifted me up as if I were a featherweight and we spun in a tiny, silent revolution to mark the moment. Him in rolled–up, yellow shirtsleeves, for which he had definitely lost the cufflinks, and brown trousers made to seem almost worn-through by careful rubbing with transparent soap. The happiness in his eyes. A victory for minor characters everywhere. Be here, I reminded myself, as he did a pirouette in his moustache and brogues. He took giant, sideways steps, pointing at the props tables and coat rails, whispering, 'You hear that, Mama? They laughed!' I couldn't wait to tell Jacqui.

When I heard the deputy stage manager give the five-minute warning to Front of House for the interval, I made my way up to Wardrobe. On the other side of the pass, the bar staff would be preparing for the rush, followed by complaints about queues for the ladies' toilets, which gave us a longer break, but also delayed us getting out at the end of the night. Margaret had decided we could cope and left us to it. Philippa came up to make a start on the laundry from the first half and to sit down for a bit. She had her book, I had mine, and it suited us both to be briefly asocial.

The noise of the outer door being pushed so hard it banged off the wall broke the silence.

'Bowe just called me "a fucking moron" in front of the whole company.' Jacqui stormed in with a tea towel in one hand and a cup in the other. She slammed the cup on the draining board and threw the tea towel on the ground in front of the washing machines.

'What happened?' Philippa asked.

'He told me to get champagne glasses for his guests and I said I don't know where they are kept. Carol is the only one who spoke up. She said, "If it's your production, Mr Bowe, then you should know where the champagne glasses are," and he thought that was hilarious.'

'Pissed,' Philippa said. 'He won't remember it. Next time he sees you, he'll offer you a job as his new publicist. Why was he backstage?'

'Fundraising, throwing his weight around, being an arsehole. Take your pick.'

'Should I tell Margaret?' I asked.

They turned to look at me for a moment, then turned back to each other.

'Didn't even get a fucking cup of tea,' Jacqui raged.

I gripped my mug a bit tighter as she surveyed the area around the sink and then the work table, still decorated with cotton-wool balls, where Philippa and I sat.

'Where's the rest of the chocolate I bought?' Jacqui asked.

The table was too busy with fabric, tools, plastic boxes of fastenings, elastic and the contents of Jacqui's handbag for me to see clearly. I made a gesture of picking up a roll of Wundaweb and searching underneath it.

'Mairéad, did you eat it? It's like being back at school.

I can't leave anything down but it's stolen. I just wanted one piece of chocolate before the cocking second half.'

I felt like I was being singled out in the playground for wetting the bed.

'Why are you here, Mairéad? You're practically bovine. Why don't you ever share anything? It's always me telling you about my life. Why don't you tell us about yours? Fucking— Fuck this place! I fucking hate it here.'

Jacqui had invented sex. She did. It was her trump card. When she wanted me to confide in her, it was to outdo me in sex stories. What I wanted to talk about was not what she would have been interested in hearing. Why was I in London? I pictured myself on a tightly packed Tube with hands groping me, moving under my shirt with dirty nails. I swallowed the images.

'Jacqui, I'm sorry Oliver was a bollocks to you, but stop taking it out on me.' I stood up and put my hands on my waist as I breathed steadily in and out. 'Ron struggles with his cravat,' I said. 'And Sandra needs more hairpins.'

'Avoid the Reception Room,' Philippa said. 'Bowe won't go back to the auditorium until they start lowering the house lights.'

Jacqui had given up on asking me to stay for a drink after work. I used to, in the early days, but it meant missing the last Tube home. 'Stay at mine,' she'd say and I'd think, Yes, I can walk to Kentish Town, no problem. What would actually happen was: 'So-and-so knows a place we can go. Share a taxi with us. Come on. Live a little.' She didn't seem to need to sleep and I had rapidly given up on that torture. However, I did miss what was said: 'Just between you and me, sweetie.' The whispers that were not secret, not really. Sandra Long, our Sonya, was especially sharp. She had invited me to a party in her Camden flat after a Saturday preview. There were large cushions on the floor, where she sat cross-legged, tapping a cigarillo into a covered ashtray on a low coffee table and sipping whisky before a handful of actors, a few crew members and the roulette guest – someone who had been at the show and hung around the edge of the group – a politician's husband, a promoter, a second cousin of someone in the cast who didn't know when to go home. There was a man in a bespoke suit that night, something with property or trading. I didn't bother to pay attention to his job, but I did notice his clothes. Double cuffs. Vintage glass frames. Silk-rose buttonhole, same as Uncle Vanya. Sandra toyed with him.

'What would you do,' she asked him, 'if you saw an actress being harassed at the bar?'

'At the St Leonard, do you mean? I have never seen anything of the kind. If I did, I would disapprove entirely, of course.'

'I see. You would disapprove. Purse your lips and frown, perhaps? Take a step back? I bet that makes a difference.'

'Far more women – older women, I mean – harass young men, you know. That, I have seen.'

Sandra spoke clearly, holding up her smoking hand. 'What companies do they run, these older women? What jobs will the young men get if they offer up their peachy arses?'

'That smacks of "hell hath no fury". You know, if you don't mind my saying—'

'I was hired because I'm fat, sweetheart. It's what they

wanted. Please don't be boring and tell me if I lost some weight, I'd actually be quite pretty; if I didn't drink so much, if I didn't talk so much . . . What about you? Haven't you ever wanted to get in on the action and behave like the other boys in the room? Plant your hands or your mouth on someone who stands still for long enough?'

She was talking about the people who went drinking with Oliver in order to stay in work and, I realised, because they enjoyed the benefits of being in the club.

10.30 p.m.

Over the headsets, a technician said, 'Come on, love, surprise us. Fall in your light for once,' in response to his final 'Go' cue.

I mouthed Sonya's 'We shall rest' speech in tandem with Sandra's performance; she had the full attention of the staff in the wings or listening to the Tannoy, or Front of House watching the monitors. They sprang into action the second the applause broke: house lights went up, auditorium doors opened and the clearing out began.

It suited me to finish the last few tasks on my own. Going through the routine of sorting the washing with my eyes half-closed, before Security came to kick me out so they could lock up. I wanted to get it done and get home without having to make conversation.

The red welt on my arm made the whole limb feel swollen and stingy. I was too tired to cook but my headache meant I needed to eat. The house would be empty. Hannah was having dinner at her mother's in High Wycombe. Which meant I did not have to endure her sitting on her boyfriend's lap, hanging from his neck like a garland, a gigantic baby, with her head on his chest and drooling when she fell asleep in front of the telly.

I was certain Hannah was glad not to have to spend the evening with me either. She seemed irritated by my presence, frowning whenever she saw me, and I was jealous she was having her dinner made for her. Samira would be out. She was friendly, but not interested in being friends. She was interested in nightclubs and finding a boyfriend and knew at first sight that I was not. Her parents lived next door and I wondered if they had bought a second house because they wanted to keep her close. We crossed paths every so often in the kitchen. Dessert was the only thing I saw her eat, usually a small scoop of chocolate ice cream in a glass bowl, sitting with her feet up on another chair and leaving the back door open while she smoked a cigarette.

'Can you take them, if my father comes in?' she said to me one night, pointing at the box on the table.

'The cigarettes? Why?'

'You don't know many Muslims, do you?'

Samira had turned away to exhale a grey cloud of tar. The longest we spent together was after 11 September 2001. She'd stayed in and asked, 'Would you mind watching Trevor McDonald with me?'

We had sat on the edge of the wicker sofa, bewildered by the news reports of multiple terrorist attacks. Her mobile phone rang a lot and she would tell whomever was on the other end, 'No, no, I can't. I'm watching Trevor now.'

'They'll bomb the Tube, won't they?' she said.

I didn't agree or disagree. I was trying not to think about it. There were limits to what I could dwell on and this was one. Travelling on the underground wasn't optional, not if I wanted to stay in work.

I walked at a clip to Green Park station, raced around the supermarket beside it that was not super; it stocked expensive fruit and wine for the residents of Mayfair and Park Lane. I picked up noodles, dried figs, milk, spinach, bag of peanuts, bread, cheddar, cereal, honey, bag of popcorn, eggs and apples. As I placed the food on the conveyor belt leading up to the till, I dropped a fistful of change and watched it roll under the unit. I got down on my hands and knees, skirting under the rubber seal with my fingers, into the dust and cornflake grit, and searched for my precious coins. Found one pound more than I had dropped and took it as a great victory.

Down and down the stairs, corridors and escalators to the Jubilee line for Kingsbury. The damp smell. Someone pushed past me, running for the Piccadilly line. The wind from the tunnel turned my snot black and the fluorescent lights inside the carriage gouged at my eyes, compounding my headache. Gently rocking. To avoid the advertisements I had not asked for or wanted to see, I stared at the map. Two men to my right. One in corduroy and desert boots, shoelaces untied; the other in dark denim and loafers. Denim and Loafers was talking.

'. . . when she was with me, and I'm just saying, because it surprised me, but she loved it that way. From behind, I mean. Well, you know what I mean.'

Corduroy Man pinched the fabric of his trousers repeatedly, like pulling out invisible pins, and kept his head down. Denim and Loafers leaned back, spreading wider, smiling. I wanted to call him out for being a prick. And probably lying. He didn't mention residue, burning, cystitis, haemorrhoids. HPV. Faecal incontinence. I clenched my anal sphincters and shook my head to wipe

77

away the image. Opened my book. Virginia Woolf. A story about a woman on a train, 'never utterly unconscious of the cheapness of eggs'. My cheese sandwich was in my bag, but I would not eat on the Tube. More germs than the inside of a toilet bowl, said the free-sheet newspaper. Hair. Mites. Gases. Microbes. Skipped forward to read 'Mrs Dalloway in Bond Street'. Thought of the dancing scenes, the ballrooms, the garden parties, the ladies in gloves. The two men got out. A mother with a tartan-patterned plastic laundry bag and her small child got on and took their seats. They were out late. Was she as tired as I was? A large shawl covered her head and shoulders, red-and-black houndstooth, like the markings of a goldfinch. I wanted to tap her elbow, ask permission to examine the material with my fingers, rest my head on the cloth and tell her I loved the strong colours. Not in London. You face front in London.

The hunger pangs were getting worse, but I was too conscious of people looking at me in the carriage, on the platforms, on CCTV, from the windows of their sardine rows of red-bricked houses. Someone was always looking at you in this city. His fingertips touching my chin, and me frozen in place. A fucking kilt. I felt angry at myself for wanting to eat.

When I closed the front door behind me, I imagined for a second I was back in Ireland where my mother was in the kitchen and would be glad to see me. I could telephone her, ask if she'd ever met a Rollo in all her earthly days? But I'd probably say something short-tempered with tiredness and upset her and leave her feeling helpless. Shoes off. Make a cup of tea. While the kettle was boiling, I started eating, slowly, taking items from the plastic bags, loading an unhealthy mixture of one thing after another into my mouth, chewing without thinking. For over an hour, I continued. Until I felt sick and scared and unable to move. He had put his hands on my shoulders. It seemed like an impossible thing, desire. To want to want to be touched.

I had told my parents I couldn't make it home last Christmas. Not for a Tuesday. If it had been a Sunday maybe, or even a Monday, I could have travelled. But not a Tuesday: show on the 24th, show on the 26th. What I didn't say was, I had sought out a short run and found one in Battersea Arts Centre, because it suited me to avoid the force-feeding, binge-drinking, wholehearted torture of going back. Relentless in their expectations that I was living it up in London and had the stories to match. I had snoozed in bed for most of the 25th, getting up to eat a delicious takeaway curry, and then going back to sleep.

The voicemail from my mother was still unopened.

My mobile phone lived in my jacket pocket, unless I took it out at work to charge it. Talking on the phone was not something I enjoyed. I pictured the cost per minute increasing like numbers on a digital clock. But the message might be important. I unlocked it and started pushing the buttons to get to the recording. What if she wanted to come over? She had loved everything about London on her short visit last year, said she wished she had emigrated when she'd had the chance. I could sleep on the floor again for a couple of nights, eat roasted chestnuts on Westminster Bridge, drink coffee in the V&A tearooms with echoes banging off the tiles, tiles like an Anatolian carpet, making you dizzy if you stared too long. Let her come. We wouldn't fight.

'Hello, it's me. I suppose you're working? You're always working. I can never get a hold of you. You might call your mother sometime. I'm glad you got away, but there's no need to vanish altogether.'

I deleted the message.

Good Friday, 29 March 2002

An intruder woke me. I felt something move across my face and then I was being smothered. Scared, really scared. Harry Adley was standing at the end of the bed in a pale linen suit, hands in his pockets. Took me a minute to come out of it, to realise I was hallucinating. There was nothing at the end of the bed, apart from the shadow of an open wardrobe door – 3.30 a.m., said the clock–radio. Sleep. Go back to sleep. My seams bursting open. In front of them. Covering the gap with my hand. To suppress the urge to vomit, I pictured myself painting a black room white as I curled into a ball and pulled the covers over my head. The advertisements at Finchley Road to remove nipple hair in special-offer, laser-therapy sessions blended with images of oral sex and everything that came out of orifices, and I was not going back to sleep. Pressure from my full bladder started to hurt and I rolled out of my nest and went to the loo.

I couldn't clean the bathroom; it would wake the house. I could listen to my mixtapes, but I was sick of my mixtapes. I could listen to the radio, but it would be English news, English weather. One language, one story. I went back to my bedroom and applied another layer of burn cream. As I lay down and waited for it to soak in, I deliberately pictured the fluffy chicks I had found in the barn one summer – sweet little puffs of baby yellow. The eggs I was collecting for Granny were left behind and I brought a newborn to her instead. I was delighted that she was delighted with me for bringing her luck. Even when she asked me to take it back to the barn and get her some eggs. She was making potato cakes to eat with savoy cabbage and sausages. Cold hands make good pastry, she told me, so pastry became my job. Holidays at her house were long days of boredom, waiting for my cousins to join me, for something to happen. The chicks were something. The horse was also something. An old grey mare that stood in the field with two beech trees. I tore up red clover and masses of ditch grass to feed her. She would take her time to come over to the fence, swishing her tail, until her breath was close and warm as blood, tickling the grass from my palm, me almost losing my balance with happiness. Her gigantic grey nostrils, the grooved yellow and blackened teeth, the pink flesh of her tongue were awful and wonderful. I'd lean forward, trying to rub the broad bone of her face or the muscle under her mane. She would turn her head to the side, keeping one eye fixed on mine. Bits of her hair caught on the barbed wire like white moss, picked out by songbirds for insulation. The scent of the roses. I wanted a cottage-pink petal to rub. Moving my finger and thumb in tiny orbits around each other, the softness between them like the floppy ears of a puppy, the belly of a piglet, the short feathers of a jackdaw's head, a horse's muzzle.

My grandmother would tell me to sit up straight at

the table and rapped hard on my knuckles with the back of her teaspoon because I shattered the top of a boiled egg with the back of mine, instead of slicing it open with a knife, like she did. I liked smashing it, the same way I would smash thin ice with the tips of my shoes. This was bad manners. I wanted to tell her to close her mouth when she was chewing, to conceal the liquid noises of her saliva and the pulp of her food, like I did. I saw her break a chicken's neck – a twist and a click. Then pluck and pluck and pluck the thick needle-tips of its feathers, starting from the headless nub, lilting as the blood hardened under her nails and down floated around her. She taught me that knitting was knotting, repeated patterns of knots until you had a garment. My mother should teach me how to use a sewing-machine, she said. My mother was too busy, I replied. What I meant was, it would only lead to a row. Granny crocheted mini juliet caps for Olwen and me, and I wore mine every Sunday that summer.

It was too warm in my room. I pushed the duvet to the edge of the bed and lay on top of the sheets. Scott Gilbourne was surely not losing sleep over yesterday. Raving about his new job, but not to me.

I fell asleep at 5 a.m. and stayed unconscious for three hours.

Forty minutes to get from the house to Bond Street Tube station. I stood on Oxford Street watching shutters coming up on department stores with five levels of escalators leading to hundreds and hundreds of square metres of shopping. The severe lighting and loud music made me want to fake my own death rather than go inside.

My mother's voice came into my head: 'Why don't you make an effort?' I followed red-and-white signs proclaiming *Sale now on* to a first-floor display of disabling heels and cheap flats, hung in matching pairs on a rack. There was one pair of black, patent-leather loafers in my size. For ten quid. Get them, get them, get them. And get out.

A mini-market beside a set of pedestrian lights had a bargain bin at the entrance. Of course it did. I bought chocolate digestives to replace what I'd eaten yesterday. Two packets. And another lemon swiss roll. Then zigzagged down through shady Soho. Cockney accents loading and unloading for fruit and veg stalls, my sex shop, the French bakery, the Spanish wine bar, weird boutiques and narrow windows. Much better. A mother and daughter holding hands passed me on Charing Cross Road. The daughter skipped along in shoes with Velcro straps across the uppers. The mother in a padded jacket and horsey boots.

The Wardrobe diary was lying open on the table. A page a day of things to be fixed. Jacqui's final note from last night was: *New heel tips needed on Ms Parker's T-bar travelling shoes.* I tried on the ten-quid loafers. Fuckit all to hell. They were too tight. Bastard things. I shouted at them, then filled them with plastic bags of water and put the creatures in the freezer box, hoping the water would expand enough to stretch them.

In dressingroom number four, I searched for stray sweat-, make-up-, blood-stained clothes that had not been collected last night. Checked the collars, cuffs, seams and groins of what was on the rails for wear and tear. Checked the notes attached by the actors saying, *Too tight*; *Too loose*. Found lost tights, hankies, hairbands, grips, pins, gloves and socks. The countertop below the large mirrors was loaded with hats, brushes, good-luck cards, magazines, open bags of sweets, bottled water, throat lozenges, mouthwash, mugs, photos, dead flowers, bottles of alcohol. The mess of it. I was grinding my teeth. I wondered if it bothered Anya as much as me.

There were four empty clothes rails to refill with clean outfits. Put on the next wash. Collect from dressingroom number five. Suits and shirts. Linen jackets, cravats, waistcoats. I gave Professor Serebryakov's car coat a once-over for any damage, but mostly I was admiring the cut. What if I tried on his travelling outfit here? Why not? If womenswear depressed me, why not try menswear? I shut the door, standing with my back to it in case someone did come in, and took off my black jeans. Hesitated for a moment because I hadn't washed the costume pieces, but they were hardly worn, one short scene at the end. Took a deep breath and pulled up the plaid trousers with their flattering, inward-facing pleats, buttoned the double-breasted waistcoat with pocket fob and added his paisley scarf to complete the look. I was certain the geometry of it, like the placement of characters on a stage, would show everything in proportion in a way that womenswear had never done for me. I wanted to be thrilled by my reflection and walked into the middle of the room to admire myself. The sight that hit me was boxy and mute. Straight up and down, nothing nipped in, not revealing or communicating anything. Apart from the masses of material hanging like curtains around the backside, making it seem enormous. It was not liberating. I did not resemble Patti Smith or feel powerful or sexy or anything positive and I stripped off faster than my fastest quick-change. Breathless and sad, I got back into my own clothes and left without checking myself in the mirror.

The list of tasks put me off eating. There were understudy rehearsals in Hammersmith next week. They would need duplicates prepared. I kept going with the washing, steaming, ironing, labelling, coming closer and closer to cleanliness until the disappointment of the morning lifted. New heel tips on the travelling shoes. When I got to that point, it meant I was leaving the building for a break before the evening shift. The treats I had bought earlier were talking to me. Two packets of biscuits? I took one to the Green Room and left it there. The second one, I would gift to the cobbler. Take it out of my sight. Not the swiss roll though, not that. I imagined eating it later, putting my feet up with the fire door open to let the light in. Then I imagined where it would spread in my body, where the additives and preservatives would sit for years to come.

The good thing about being busy was, it distracted me from thinking about my arm. I replaced the burn cream, in case someone else came looking for it. A pregnancy smock for Mae Pollitt in *Cat on a Hot Tin Roof*. That was the last time I'd burned myself properly. The scar it had left on my wrist was fading.

4.30 p.m.

After the drop-off at the cobbler's, I started walking downhill until I had to stop at the bottom of Trafalgar Square. Diesel from black cabs, red buses and the constant traffic coming from the six or seven roads leading to the roundabout made me think about what I was absorbing through my skin and lungs. I had to take a moment to figure out where I wanted to go and how many crossings it would take to get there. The decision was made for me as one set of lights changed and I moved with a large group of pedestrians to a concrete island in the middle of the road. Closing my eyes briefly, I imagined grey clouds massing over Ben Bulben and the smell of cedar and gorse after rain. The white flash of a hare's tail. What Jacqui said last night: 'Why are you here?' As if it had not occurred to me.

With the momentum of the crowd around me, I made it to the top of Whitehall and thought about walking towards the river. The day I arrived in London, I came to see Big Ben. From Westminster Tube station, I had wandered around Parliament Square, ambling across to the Houses of Parliament. The first statue I stopped at was Oliver Cromwell. The shock and then the rage that had overtaken me when I read his name: my hands tightened into fists and I might have growled. I certainly curled my lips. When they taught us history in primary school, his name went hand in glove with siege, massacre and burning us alive. The concept of building a statue to him was not within my understanding. It would be like celebrating the arrival of mass starvation.

I changed tack. Not in the direction of Westminster or the river, but down the Mall to walk across St. James's Park. I had not set foot in London before I moved here. Flying from Dublin to Heathrow Airport with a large blue rucksack. The weight of it made me tip forward as I went from the terminal to the underground, crossing the city in tunnels dug by navvies. I was not a city person, yet here I was exchanging a small one for a metropolis.

My new landlord had met me outside Kingsbury Tube station.

'Mah-rayad?' he asked.

I was astonished by him. How did he know me? How long had he been waiting? Whatever worries I had about coming here faded as he spoke.

'The rucksack,' he said, gesturing to my turtle curve. 'Would you like me to take it?'

'No, thank you,' I said. 'Thank you for coming to meet me, Mr Hanif.' I pronounced it like Hanaffy.

'Ha-níf,' he corrected me. 'But please call me Shadaan.' He put his hand over his heart and I found myself affirming his nod of 'yes' with my own. We were agreed. With an opening of his arm, he guided me down the street and we walked together to his house where a meal had been prepared for me. Oven chips and Coca-Cola. A woman stood as I entered the kitchen, hands clasped over her stomach.

'Fatima,' Mr Hanif said. 'My wife.'

'Sit,' Fatima told me, pulling out a chair. 'Shadaan will take your bag.' She sat close beside me. This was not what I had learned to expect from landlords. They could not know I would struggle with the food. Coke was paint stripper, according to my mother, and packet food with unrecognisable ingredients would lead to heart disease. Their kindness, however, was more important. I sat and put a chip into my mouth, wide-eyed, hearing myself chewing.

'Do you like our new window?' Fatima asked me.

There was a large, double-glazed window over the sink, facing onto a back garden with apple trees.

'We were almost robbed,' Fatima continued. 'They took the old window out, the whole window, in broad daylight, and were climbing into our home.'

'I was here,' Shadaan said. 'I heard them.' He must have noticed my jaw dropping. 'It's all fixed now – everything new and very secure,' he said quickly, beaming at the double-glazing with raised locks on each handle. 'I will take your bag to your room. Come next door when you are ready.'

'My room is next door?' I asked.

I was taking the room of an Irish girl who had recently left; a drama-school student who was the sister of a production manager in Dublin. The production manager of my last show there. 'The solutions will come when you need them,' she had said, giving me the contact details for Mr Hanif.

'Yes. The bedroom at the front. The others are at

work. Hannah, she is a civil servant, and Samira, my daughter. Samira is an accountant. In Central London.' Shadaan picked up my bag and nodded 'yes' again. I raised myself out of the chair. He dropped the bag and waved his hands to stop me.

'No, no, stay, please. Eat.'

I sat back down, twirling the fork in my hand. The cola bubbles fizzed in the glass, untouched.

'You would like to relax, after your journey?' Fatima smiled at me.

'I might go back to the city centre. To Central London, I mean. To look around?'

I had called my mother from a payphone in the under-ground shopping centre at Bond Street station.

'Here, fine, no problems. Haven't seen anything yet, but I'm getting the Tube to Westminster, down to the river.' Elated. Dying to explore.

'Say hello to Big Ben from me,' she said.

7 p.m.

I was late. Walked too far in the wrong direction and got badly lost trying to find a shortcut back, ending up in cul-de-sacs instead. This city would puncture any notion that I knew where I was going. The evening staff had already opened the foyer to the public. I went in by the front doors, hoping to get up through the building quickly. Mildew Miller was on the other side of the pass to the backstage areas, coming towards me. Typical coward, always looking for a woman on her own. On the day after the opening-night celebrations, he had crept up behind me while I was at the sewing-machine, concentrating on keeping a seam straight. From nowhere, I felt a sharp pressure on my windpipe, like a cheese wire about to cut through rind. He had bridled a length of cotton thread across my throat and was silently pulling on it from behind. It was only the beginning of the run, too soon to be murdered. I knew who it was and sat motionless, trying to focus on the stacks of clear plastic boxes filled with buttons and fasteners on the shelves opposite. The pressure increased and he had leaned close to my ear.

'Just checking you haven't lost your sense of humour,' he said.

I remembered how he had stretched across the bar counter, trying to separate me from the person I was chatting to, and crooned, 'So, tell me about yourself, Miss Sweeney.'

'No,' I said, walking away. Creeps do not seem to notice how obvious they are. Or that pretending to garrotte someone will not make them like you. He was Venue Staff Supervisor, employed by the St Leonard, and had surely figured out how to keep his job while starting a whispering campaign against me. The thing to do was to wait for him to get bored and leave, which he did. The fear didn't arrive until the next time I saw him. Even though he had performed his strangulation trick from behind, what came into my mind was the look on his face as he did it. It slowed my blood whenever he surfaced. I swear he waited in the narrow corridors and alcoves in order to press close to junior staff, forcing them to squeeze past. He smelled, to me, of mildew.

'Oh, excuse me. Sorry. Ha-ha. May I have this dance?' Hands on my waist, moving downwards, before resting on my hips. 'Alluring this evening, aren't we, Miss Sweeney?'

After he spoke, I heard him sniff, while I tried to flatten myself to the wall. He was sucking an apple drop, rattling the boiled sweet like a marble in his mouth. He was too strong to push away, and if I did, he would repeat the version of events that suited him best. Most likely, 'She can't take a joke.'

There were heavy footsteps coming from the direction of Front of House. Clive. In his combat trousers. Carrying a phase tester instead of a stepladder. Mildew dropped his hands and I fixed my eyes on Clive while sliding further along the wall to get to the stairwell.

'Charlotte in Box Office is looking for you, Richard,' Clive said.

Clive kept his body between me and Mildew, watching until we heard the coded door to the public side of the building open and then lock shut. I started walking upstairs.

'All right?' he asked after me.

'Yep, thank you,' I replied, without turning around, because I hadn't the energy to start crying. In the stairwell, I rubbed my eyes with my fists, wanting to scream or smash a stack of plates. It was something and nothing. It was too often to take seriously. It didn't matter to anyone else.

'Listen to this!' Jacqui came in waving a newspaper. She held up a Q&A feature with 'fearless' West-End actor Scott Gilbourne.

'Says he doesn't eat before a show. Well, that's true. Afraid of shitting himself at the five-minute call, probably. Says he walks out psychically naked, attuned to the audience, that every performance is unique. "This is not a stepping-stone towards the big one, the better one: everything is now, in this moment." But he is in the paper because of the cocking BBC thing, not what he is actually doing, "now, in this moment".'

'Must be nice for him,' I said. 'Striving for those heights while someone else cleans his hair from the plugholes.'

'He never listens to how I say things to him. Is an actor not trained to notice how you say, "Oh, no, of course I love this job"?' Jacqui did not appear to be talking to me. She tore out the page from the newspaper and pinned it to the noticeboard.

'Our one-way relationships.' Philippa was crouching in front of the open fridge door. She had already sorted the dry-cleaning and was putting away her food for later. 'They don't want you to talk about your problems. Mairéad, why are there shoes in the freezer?' She held up my monsters.

'I'm trying to stretch them,' I said. 'Unlike Ms Parker, I can't— Oh, Jesus H. Christ. Her shoes. Fuck, fuck, fuck!'

Philippa's face, looking at my face, instantly realised what I had done. The cobbler's shop was closed. 'Stop what you're doing.' She did not panic, unlike me, but was visibly calculating options. 'Give me your list. Jacqui and I will do the preset. Margaret is in her office. You have to tell her first and then find a replacement. We could have an unreturned pair from a shopping trip. Or there might be something in the understudy set? We can check the stores.'

'Philippa. Thank you.'

Margaret's door was open, but I knocked and waited for her permission to enter. My throat was a scratched, narrow pipe. I told her I had not collected the shoes. They were locked in the shoe-repairs shop.

'This is a disaster. You have created an absolute disaster.'

'I'm on my way to the stores.'

'We don't have stores; this isn't the bloody National. Have you no idea how we work? Do you think we found her shoes in a backstage cupboard?' Margaret threw a manila folder past my head, slapping the wall behind me. 'Find Ms Parker. Tell her. No, don't tell her yet. Go to her dressingroom, see what shoes are in there and if there is something we can use before you tell her.'

Would she have spoken to Philippa like that? I didn't know Margaret was finished speaking until she shouted: 'Go!'

I could smell Ms Parker from outside her dressingroom. Cigarettes, peppermint, expensive perfume. Already here. I knocked twice and waited for her to say 'Come in' before I opened the door. She was sitting with her feet up on a stool, reading, sipping a hot drink, and did not look up.

'Your shoes.' Sweat was beading across my forehead and at the nape of my neck. I was unable to come up with an excuse to go in and go through her existing collection.

'Yes?'

'The travelling shoes. I—'

Ms Parker placed a postcard between the open pages of her book. 'Didn't you get them mended?'

'No, I did. I took them out this morning.'

'All right, then. Thank you.' She lifted up the postcard and resumed reading.

'I forgot to collect them.' If I concentrated on her face, it would help me to go on. 'I've only just realised, I'm so sorry. They'll have closed by now. Which means I've created a disaster. And . . . I'm . . . It's my—' My name would be in tonight's show report. Noting how Ms Parker had to go out barefoot in act four owing to Mairéad Sweeney's incompetence.

Ms Parker closed her book and sighed. 'I see.' She watched me for a moment as I pressed the back of my hand to my forehead. 'Are they getting their knickers in a twist upstairs? Come on, darling, buck up. Worse things happen at sea. Find a solution. The audience won't notice, I promise you.'

The Ronettes were playing on the Tannoy. It was 7.20 p.m. The show would begin in forty minutes and Jacqui would have to use something. I pictured Yelena's costumes from what was laid out backstage: swing dress, capri pants, embroidered cardigan, sheath dress; cream, pink, green; broad collars, mushroom hat, swing coat, ankle strap or kitten heels or wedges.

'The wedges,' I blurted out, 'from act one – the nude wedges. Could they work? They would blend with the colour of the travelling coat.'

Ms Parker inclined her head and pursed her lips. 'For one night.'

'I'll have to go back and clear it with the others.'

'You can use the nude wedges, Jacqui,' I said, 'instead of the travelling shoes.'

Jacqui and Philippa stopped what they were doing as I walked back into the room and went straight to the kitchen sink.

'Does Margaret know?' Philippa asked.

'What did Alison say?' Jacqui asked.

'Yes, she knows.' The blank stare Margaret had given me made me feel like an imbecile. 'Ms Parker agreed, just for tonight.' My hands shook as I picked up the kettle and filled it from the cold tap. 'I need a cup of tea.'

Turing around to look at them, I leaned against the edge of the stainless-steel ridge and folded my arms across my chest. 'I think it was because I was down near

96

Westminster on my break. Thinking about Cromwell and then the Famine. That was why I forgot to collect the shoes.'

They were both staring at me. Philippa held a needle in one hand, frozen in place.

'The famine in Malawi?' Jacqui asked.

I did not know about the famine in Malawi.

'No, in Ireland,' I said.

The water beginning to heat was the only sound in the room. If I wasn't so confused, I would have laughed.

'There's a famine in Ireland?' Jacqui had her bag on the table. Its open mouth faced me.

'*The* Famine,' I said. 'The Irish Famine. In the 1840s?' I was gobsmacked.

Jacqui took the lid off a tube and began rubbing cream onto the back of her hands. 'The 1840s? What has that got to do with the shoes?'

'The event that killed, that exiled, more than half of the population? The government policies, massive emigration, losing our language?' I halted. Had I been brainwashed? Had she?

Jacqui continued to massage her pale hands, wearing a vintage black-jersey dress, covering her sweatshop underwear. Philippa. Who would forever win the competition to be the last one to finish eating, as if she were made of bird bones and not an adult female with a stomach. I wanted to strip away their homes, their security, their choice to stay where they were reared. My great-great-grandparents. My mother. No money to send her to secondary school. It was so long ago. It was yesterday. I remembered a woman in a porter's uniform in Waterloo station, sweeping litter into a long-handled dustpan, and I asked her if there was a bin nearby. 'No,' she said, snapping the lid of the dustpan shut, 'because of the IRA.' How was I supposed to summarise what I did not fully understand?

The kettle reached boiling point and switched off automatically. It had nothing to do with forgetting the shoes. Was I or was I not doing the same job as Philippa and Jacqui? Then what did it matter if they knew about the 1840s in Ireland?

'Rambling from St. James's Park to Hyde Park while daydreaming is what happened.' I held up three mugs and their smiles at being waited on felt like a knife in my side. Turning away from them, I added a teabag to each cup and poured the hot water. 'Wasn't it nice, the way your father came to collect you at Christmas, Philippa? Drove you to Bristol, I think you said. Your homeplace?'

'Bath.' Her tone was flat and cold. 'Two very different places.'

This from the woman who thinks there is only one location in Ireland — Dublin — and then looks impatient when there are other placenames. 'Is that near Dublin?' she would ask. I was about to dig in again, ask her about what she ate, Any peasant children on the menu? But Jacqui interrupted me.

'Shut up, sweetie.'

'What did I say?' The affront gave me the energy to face her, willing them to pick a fight. 'I only asked about Christmas. Can we not ask about Christmas now?'

Philippa turned away from me and rubbed her cheek. 'My father came to collect me because I told my mother that my boyfriend said I wasn't spending Christmas with anyone but him and then he punched me. I was living in his place, so it was quite awkward for everyone.'

Jacqui glanced over at Philippa and turned back to admonish me. 'Now stop being a cunt, darling.'

I gave up on making the drinks. The aggression of a man begging outside the Tube station last week came back to me. He had horrible teeth and religious beads around his neck. 'Five pounds,' he kept saying, 'I need five pounds for a burger and chips.'

I'd shouted 'No' viciously at him as he followed me along the street.

'I'm cold,' he had wailed.

Last night's broken sleep, forgotten all day, rose up and flung itself against my back, pulling me downwards.

Philippa continued patching a hole in the lining of a jacket sleeve and didn't speak. The tea was stewing. I stared at the liquid in each mug, paralysed with fatigue. The thought that she could be bullied, be anything but composed and sure of herself, stunned me.

'I'm sorry, Philippa. I didn't mean to . . . I . . . But . . . So.'

'Sit down with us, please, Mairéad,' Jacqui said, 'while we have two minutes. I'll finish the tea.'

There was nothing to occupy my hands. I sat with my fingers interlaced, wondering how to get through this evening. If I could say something, it might help.

'Philippa,' I said, meaning to apologise properly, then hesitating as she lifted her needle high in the air and her face hardened. I remembered the picture of the French aristocrat on her swing, one toe pointed and raised. 'Before women wore underpants, or a closed crotch and gusset, I mean—'

'Hang on,' Jacqui interrupted, 'why did no one tell me this before? Were they actually all long-skirts-and-no-knickers?'

I reached out to where Jacqui stood at the sink and then put my palm flat on the table. 'Yes,' I said, and raised a finger to hold my place. I was going to say this without stumbling, like an efficient nurse, unafraid of bodily fluids. 'What did they wear during their period?'

'I don't know.' Philippa thought it over.

'How fabulous. It must have felt wonderful.' Jacqui placed a cup of tea next to me and remained standing to drink her own.

'In the whole wide world of women, no descriptions, no patterns?' I couldn't articulate it, how incredible it was to me.

Philippa was calmer. 'I haven't read everything, Mairéad.' Her half-smile lifted my heart. 'There is a lot of advice, in old housekeeping manuals, you know. "How to remove grease with lye." I suspect they meant blood. Blood, sweat.'

'And sperm,' Jacqui added loudly.

'It's difficult enough to remove fake blood from anything,' Philippa continued, unfazed.

'Except black,' I said.

'They could have attached something to a foundation garment,' she decided, 'and were supposed to feel ashamed about it, rather than put words into print. We're so stupidly dishonest, aren't we?'

As soon as Philippa said this, the room seemed brighter. A tiny knot in my thoughts unravelled.

'I bet that's why the nuns dressed in black,' Jacqui said, 'and were locked away. Why would you bother making underwear when you could just imprison women?' A shiver ran across her shoulders and she shook it off. 'Horrible. But I do like the idea of going loosey-goosey every day. De–li–cious.' Her mobile phone buzzed with a text message and she reached into her bag to find it.

'The silence is disturbing,' I said, looking at Philippa. 'Stupidly dishonest,' I repeated, because I didn't want to forget her words.

With a dramatic pause, Jacqui pressed her phone to her chest. 'Tonight, I have to leave immediately after curtain call.' She closed her eyes for a second. 'Mairéad, could you possibly cover for me? I'll pay you back, I promise, but I really, really cannot be here.'

'Oh, of course,' I said. 'If Margaret hasn't fired me by then. Did something happen?'

'Thank you, sweetheart.' Jacqui reached out and squeezed my hand.

'I'll talk to Margaret,' Philippa said.

Jacqui took one more mouthful from her mug and left it on the table. 'I've got an audition in the morning! In Soho, which is perfect. Right, off to work we go.' As she walked down the corridor, I heard her talking into her phone: 'Mum, is that you? You'll never guess what's happened.'

The tea she had given me was cold and too strong. I poured the spoiled liquid down the sink.

At the end of the show, I was back outside Alison Parker's dressingroom. I could have said no to Jacqui. If I had said no, I would not be frozen mid-stride like a deer in headlights. Oliver Bowe had got there before me. His

101

body was so close to the door, he was either about to force his way in or it had been shut in his face. There was a sound of running water on the other side.

'Alison. For fuck's sake, this is idiotic. Open up.'

His tone was what Margaret described as Oliver's master-of-the-hunt voice. It was embarrassing, she said, to be in a restaurant or on a train with him and his need to be publicly, viciously superior. It felt like I had turned into the wrong enclosure, about to trigger a snare. My instinct was to get away before we made eye contact. Except, if I hid, how long would I have to wait? *For fuck's sake yourself, Oliver*, I wanted to hiss. I needed to collect Ms Parker's washing before I could leave the building. The plastic laundry basket under my arm, wet towels over my shoulder, my mouth open. I couldn't calculate how to get around him.

'I don't suppose you'd like to come to dinner with a brilliant venture capitalist and his teenage daughter?' He pinched his inner eye sockets and then turned his head in my direction. 'Would you?'

The skin on my arms contracted in goosebumps and tiny hairs rose on my neck.

'The daughter wants to act, you see. So,' he raised his voice and turned back to the door, 'it would have been most helpful if our female lead could have got fucking dressed in time to join us.'

There was the slightest movement, a twitch of his eyelids. 'Who is responsible for putting Ms Parker in the wrong shoes?'

I took a step backwards.

'Her final scene. Who dressed her?'

'Me,' I said.

'And you couldn't manage to get her shoes right? Are you an idiot?'

How did he know? He had been in maybe once a month since opening night, and then usually after the show. What was he doing here, two nights in a row?

'It was a mistake. I apolo—'

'Is that what Margaret is doing now? Employing idiots? Why, do you think, would we pay a designer to spend months drawing pictures of shoes and coats and ridiculously expensive hats if you know better than they do?'

'No, I—'

'No! Of course you fucking don't. You do not get to mess with my show, do you understand?'

I was no longer able to reply and stood in silence.

'Happy in your job, are you?'

The brightness startled me. It was a complete switch, a firmly major chord. I didn't move.

'Do you like your job?' he said, more slowly. 'I've seen you before, haven't I? Irish? Terribly romantic, the Irish language. Do you speak it? What's the word for a dell?'

The towels slid from my shoulder as my head bobbed like an apple in a river, swept any which way by the current. What the fuck was a dell?

'A dell,' he repeated, 'how do you say it in Gaelic?'

'Poll,' I said, gathering the towels off the floor and half-hoping a hole would open up to swallow me.

The disappointment that registered across his mouth. Jesus. I had not made the sound he expected.

'Your name?' he barked.

'Mairéad.'

'Mairéad.' Pronouncing it just as I had said it. Not 'Marmalade', not 'Mermaid', just Mairéad.

'I am surrounded by fantasists, Mairéad, who have no idea.' He exhaled as he closed his eyes. 'Where do they think the money comes from?'

It was a softly spoken plea. What I saw, with a surprising note of empathy, was a man who carried everyone's salary on his back. He thought about money, he worried about money, possibly even more than I did. How stupid of me not to realise it. We did the same labour: humouring and cajoling. He, too, was surrounded by self-absorbed egos.

'If I set up a dinner with, say, Vivienne Westwood, and asked you to come, help us to secure funding for a tour, for the benefit of the company, you'd do your bit, wouldn't you? Of course you would. Because you want the show to survive. No, it's more than that – you want it to be extraordinary. What others will try and fail to imitate.'

It felt like being hypnotised. I could not stop staring back at him. Yes, I wanted to be at that table.

'I admire how much you've done for us; don't think I haven't noticed. You'd like a pay rise, yes?' He raised his chin and I felt my eyes and throat opening wide. 'And I'd very much like to give it to you, but where would the money come from, tell me? And what would you do to get it?' His easy manner did not change as he turned his shoulders towards me. 'How would you make things more efficient? What would you cut?'

Raptors do not flap, they glide. The tightening of the muscles in his neck as he asked me to betray my colleagues. Margaret. If Margaret were here. She would have shut this down immediately. Answer his questions and I'd find myself out of a job. The running water continued.

'Excuse me, Mr Bowe, I am sorry, but I really need to collect Ms Parker's costumes.'

He didn't shout at me. Standing up straight on an inhale, I stepped closer and made to knock on the door, but he took my wrist and pressed his thumb over the vein, as if to take my pulse.

'She's showering, can't be disturbed.' Mouth curved like a crocodile, absolutely sure he was winning. 'Come and work for my office, why don't you? When you're tired of doing other people's laundry.'

He dropped my hand and strutted down the empty corridor. It shouldn't have been empty. I wondered how many others were hiding, secretly listening to us. I turned back to the door and knocked lightly. There was a measured click of a lock, followed by a scent of cigarettes, peppermint and perfume. Alison Parker's eyeball asked me, 'Is he gone?'

'Yes,' I said. 'May I come in, Ms P— Alison? To collect the laundry?'

She gathered me in one arm and spun me into the room, simultaneously pushing the door closed with her back. She had not undressed but stood clutching the hook-and-eye clasp at the collar of her coat. I would have to wait for her to take off her costume. This was all right, I told myself, this was all right, and I admired the wide swing coat that complemented the buttermilk shades and folds of the skirt underneath. Their bottom hems aligned as closely as the edges of an oyster shell, both trimmed in black ribbon to match her gloves, her mushroom hat. The gloves Margaret wanted replicated. I pictured the new pair, preset into the pocket of the coat, right thumb facing up and no one noticing they were different.

'All right,' Alison was saying, 'all right.' We could have been running lines. Her fingers loosened their grip but she did not undo the clasp. Smoker's fingers. Red sausages. Always cold.

'He will call me a cunt now, because I want to go home to my own bed.'

It wasn't clear to me if she was angry or frightened. If I tried to rush her, she might react badly. I put down my basket and asked her if she needed more towels before she got in the shower.

'Which do you think is worse: when they constantly want something from you or when they stop?' She rested her head against the door and raised her eyes to the ceiling. 'It's not really me they want, is it? Not the me that is hungry and tired after a show, asking myself what I'm doing with my life, how I will survive when I'm past it, when no one wants to hire me.' She gestured at the cards on her dressing table. 'Do you have a crush on someone?'

The directness of the question made my heart skip a beat. How did she know I had a crush on someone?

'And do you imagine them doing mundane things? Do you imagine yourself doing mundane things with them, or being bored of them, or wishing they would clean the toilet once in a while and think about someone other than themselves for five minutes? No. Thought not.' There was a steady flow of tears down the sides of her face and she did nothing to clear them away.

'Can I help you?' I said, focusing on the cashmere coat in order to keep my voice calm. Her hands relaxed and I crouched down to remove her shoes. Only she wasn't wearing shoes; she had already removed them, but remained on tiptoe in her stockinged feet, as though she had formed that way. Reversing upwards, I began to do my job, to release her as quietly and swiftly as possible. Neither of us spoke as we removed the layers of her fastenings together. The valuable women, I reminded myself, had no capacity to carry a sword. She stepped out of the lines and curves that had encased her and walked naked into the windowless alcove they called a bathroom. The shower water had been running for so long, I worried it would be stone-cold. They should have dressed her in kingfisher blue; it's what I thought every time I saw her in this outfit, and rigged the stage lights to show it off. Her clothes held the shape of her torso like a wren's nest: the frame of her shoulders, the breast moulds, her waist, the places where she had pushed and pulled her character through one more repetition, one more performance. Sweating it out, a damp trace left on the silk. We put up signs in the dressingrooms asking actors to separate their dress shields from their clothes and put them in the laundry bin provided. Alison didn't. It was all right, I told myself again, it was all right.

Philippa was buttoning up her coat when I got back to Wardrobe.

'I heard you, talking to Oliver.' She pressed her lips together and widened her eyes.

'Where were—?'

'What a night!' Undoing the bun in her hair, she tipped her head forward, displaying the nape of her neck to me, then brushed out the kinks. I couldn't talk to her with her face upside-down. She righted herself, checked nothing was caught in her collar, and picked up her bag. 'All set. See you tomorrow.'

I did not reply. She had finished her work. I was the one who'd agreed to cover for Jacqui, not her, and had no reason to be angry because she was leaving. Yet I couldn't speak. I stood with a full laundry basket in my arms, with even more costume pieces over both shoulders, and listened to Philippa's footsteps walking away. The silk of Alison's dress brushed my cheek and I imagined the sound of an ocean swell at night with a clear sky and a full moon. Saltwater could stain silk and I would miss the last Tube if I didn't shake myself.

I wiped my face with the sides of my hands and started moving quickly, throwing piles at the washing machines and another at the sink. When I went to soak the delicates, the monster loafers were looking up at me from the basin. Someone had probably put their ready-meal in the freezer and left my ten-quid, too-tight, too-ugly shoes out. The plastic bags of water I had put inside the uppers to stretch them were defrosting. I thought about throwing the shoes across the room or firing them at the skylight until it shattered. The place would be full of pigeons in the morning and I'd be on a plane to, to where? Thought dismissed, I blazed through the rest of the tasks in a frenzy and ran for the last train. Someone might have a dog with them. A sweet, soft dog next to me and I could rub its chest. I would donate the loafers. They were evidently not meant for me.

When I was leaving through the pass at Stage Door, I saw the carrier bag I had taken to the cobbler's, sitting on the countertop. The T-bar travelling shoes were inside, new tips added, nothing amiss. A note was taped to the handle: *Your cobbler said thank you for the biscuits. You can bring my biscuits tomorrow. Mr H.* Which meant they had been here before the show. Mr Henderson must have asked the evening shift to let me know. Or maybe not.

I was incredibly happy about getting home to bed and managed to fall asleep without having to eat.

Saturday, 30 March 2002

The sound of the morning alarm was submarine and my body was a rock on the seabed. As still as a corpse. I did not want to surface. Sitting on the edge of the pine-framed bed, my head was a dry-stone wall. I got up with my eyes mostly closed, feeling my way to the bathroom.

I came to on the kitchen floor, disorientated, my flatmate kneeling over me, talking on the house phone. Breakfast cereal and milk were spray-painted across the room. Hannah said, 'She's conscious now, thank you,' rang off and began addressing me.

'You fainted. I called the NHS helpline. They said if you're alert, I can put you in a cab.'

Her lips and her fingers were moving quickly, frowning as she dialled another number. The back of my head throbbed. I leaned onto my left elbow and brought the fingers of my right hand to the ridge between my skull and neck. They came back red and wet and I did not know if it was day or night, what country I was in, whether I was awake or dreaming.

I heard Hannah whisper 'Shit' and then hold music playing through the receiver as she left it on the table and pressed a wad of tissues against the cut. I had no energy to talk to her. When the hold music stopped, she ordered a minicab to take me to the hospital. As I lay on the ground, I saw the open cupboard door under the kitchen sink was hanging awkwardly, broken away from its top hinge.

Hannah was out the front, telling the driver I was coming. She got me to my feet, checked for my keys and wallet in my jacket pockets and wanted to know if I'd be all right on my own.

'Is my phone there?' I asked her.

'No,' she said. 'Shall I look upstairs, in your room?'

My head. I had to close my eyes. The mobile phone wasn't in my room. It was charging from the plug next to a sewing-machine in Wardrobe, because I'd forgotten to bring it home. 'Thanks, but it won't be up there. If it's not in my jacket, then I've left it in the theatre.'

From the way she compulsively checked her watch, I knew Hannah was getting impatient.

'Are you late for work?' I asked.

She dropped her frown and said, 'It's Saturday.' For a second, I thought she was going to question me on what year it was and who was Tony Blair. 'I'm meeting my rambling group.' The most important date in her diary. How could I have forgotten?

I wasn't slighting Hannah. I really was an idiot. It was Easter Saturday and the last Saturday of the month. Philippa was doing the prep shift before today's matinée, not me. I could have stayed in bed. Hannah guided me outside, opened and closed the car door, then told the driver to go to Casualty. Where I lied to the triage nurse, saying it had never happened before, I was not prone to fainting for no reason. But I had fainted on

112

the Tube last summer. Managed to hold on to an upright pole as I crumpled to the ground in silence, then wondered why I was waking up for the second time in one day. A man had given up his seat for me and I dropped my head between my knees, lifting the clothes off my lower back to let my skin breathe. I had tried to use my travelcard to open the coded pass door at work, but apart from that, put it to the back of my mind, where I wanted it to stay. I apologised to the nurse for wasting their time and said this was not serious, just embarrassing. The nurse believed people died of embarrassment. He cleaned the small cut on my head, took several blood samples, told me to get myself something with sugar in it and go back to the waiting room. I sipped hot, sweet tea from a vending machine and avoided sitting next to a drunken man. He was shouting, with the same accent as mine, about the bitches at the reception desk.

It was 10 a.m. and there was no way of knowing how long I'd have to wait. From a payphone in the corner, I dialled Stage Door. To my surprise, Mr Henderson said Margaret was in her office. He transferred the call.

I didn't tell her I was in a hospital. I told her I had bumped my head and might be late for work while I got it checked, but it shouldn't take long, it wasn't serious, mostly likely it was nothing at all, and she told me to stop talking and listen.

'You need to call your aunt, in Ireland. They're trying to find you because your grandmother has died.'

There was a time delay happening, like a transatlantic conversation: I could hear the words but their meaning swung out of reach for a moment. I might have said

'Right' or 'Okay' or 'What?' I might have said nothing intelligent at all.

'Sorry, darling, but I need to reorganise everyone, you understand? Don't come into work. Ask the doctor to check for concussion. And call your family.'

A bruise was blooming under my eye and my body was turning numb with shock. End one phone call. Begin another. I had only one living grandmother and I knew her number off by heart. Olwen, my cousin, picked up the receiver.

'Are you all right?'

'My boss told me.'

'There was no answer on your mobile and we couldn't find a house number. So Mum got the number of the theatre from Directory Enquiries and left two messages, and then, on the third go, the woman said you weren't there. We didn't know what to think. Maybe London had swallowed you up.'

A nurse started to call my name.

'What happened to Granny Kate?'

'Heart attack. Last night. Where are you?'

'In a hospital. For nothing. I fell over, had a fight with a cupboard door.' My mind had blanked out whatever happened. I didn't know what I had done.

'You'll have to come home.'

The calling behind me turned to shouting. 'They're looking for me. I'd better go. Sorry. I don't have my phone, but I'll be on the next flight, don't worry. Sorry.'

My test results were clear; there were no abnormalities. They had no reason to keep me in.

I returned to the house, got back on the phone and leaned against the woodchip wallpaper in the hallway until I'd booked a flight to Knock Airport. It was tight, but I'd make it. All my blacks were at the theatre, where Margaret had been left short-staffed for two shows. There wasn't time to pack carefully or to regret not being better prepared, so I flung some clothes into a bag, put on a warmer jumper for the journey and grabbed the pencil case where I kept my passport and Irish money. The cash would be useless; they'd switched to euro in January. I'd figure out what to do with it when I landed. On my way out, I wrote a note and left it on the kitchen table. The only trace of the accident was the broken door. Hannah must have cleaned up the mess.

People seemed exceptionally quiet on the trains to Stansted, flowing around me in shoals on and off the carriages and across platforms, breaking apart silently at the escalators. I could see her, standing at her kitchen door, gazing up at a white streak crossing the sky, mouth slightly open, mesmerised. Even though she had never set foot on an airplane. The sense of floating stopped abruptly when I reached the overheated departures terminal. Nausea hit me as I walked past the smoking section. The check-in attendant glanced at my passport, ripped my boarding card from the printer and stared at me. She said only one word: 'Run.'

I barrelled my way through suits, briefcases, cleaning carts, slowed down briefly through Security, pounded past brightly lit duty-free stands, shopping bags, backpacks, the kiosk with racks of paperbacks, to the gate. My lungs and heart were coming out through my skin and continued to pump blood and sweat to the surface until the seatbelt sign switched off somewhere over Hertfordshire.

Ireland

Saturday, 30 March 2002

We landed ahead of schedule. Which didn't matter, because I hadn't told anyone when I was arriving. I stopped a middle-aged couple in the foyer of the regional airport, asked them if they were driving anywhere near Charlestown. Trying to put across my most pleasant, amenable self. The woman said they could drop me off, surely. Her sister was flying back on that plane, would you believe it? The one I had just left. At the edge of the town, I hitched the first of three more lifts. A delivery man who talked about English roads and played Johnny Cash cassettes, a junior doctor with a stethoscope sliding around on the back seat as he yawned and sighed, and a young fella in his first car who just wanted to drive and drive. He told me he was an apprentice mechanic, working on a classic car with his friends. He spent all of his love and money on engines. I thought he was incredibly kind and struggled to refuse when he offered to take me right to the door of my grandmother's home. If we had gone there, I would not have been able to leave his car or his company. It was too soon. I asked him to drop me at the edge of the village of Droimnín, telling him I had something I needed to do.

My parents and my grandmother lived thirty minutes' drive from Sligo town, in opposite directions and separate counties. My parents in Donegal, my grandmother in Leitrim. Granny Kate had moved to my grandfather's farm when they married, a couple of miles from Droimnín. As I wandered down the main street, I heard her telling me to pick up my heels as we passed the rusted water pump, take my hands out of my pockets beside the post box, stop leaning over the railings at the bridge where I used to throw grass into the river, waiting for her to finish talking in the local shop and take me home.

On the other side of the bridge, there was a sharp turn at the end of the village and open countryside beyond it. I started walking. A wren flew down from a rowan tree and skimmed the lowest part of a hedge on my left, leaping ahead of my feet, warning me off its patch with the ferocity of a sewing-machine needle puncturing cotton at full speed. I'd never known a wren that wasn't spoiling for a fight; it wasn't singing so much as exploding with rage. The strap of my bag bit into my shoulder. I shifted it to the other side, shrugged it closer to my neck and squeezed my upper arms hard to push out the numbness. A spare pair of jeans, a red T-shirt and a longer blue T-shirt to sleep in. I hadn't brought a good pair of shoes. Or funeral clothes. This was a nightmare. A teenage boy cycled past with both hands in his pockets, his knees sticking out to the sides like raised middle fingers. Impulsively, I wanted to stop a passing car, ask if I could get in, sit on my fingertips to ease out the biting wind, go back in the direction I'd come from. But what if they recognised me? I stifled the impulse and kept my head down, fighting the urge to turn on my heel. My teeth started to chatter. You would think moving away would have blurred the anger and fear of a place. You would think. I was watching birds and cyclists and not managing to get anything straight.

Without planning to, I ended up at the fields with the Stone-age tombs. My aunt used to march me and my cousins up what she called the highest mountain in Leitrim, which was not high, or even a mountain, to point out ring forts and burial mounds, like ripples in the landscape. Links in a chain, she said, which is what her father had said. They appeared haphazard up close, but part of a careful pattern from above. Whoever built them had understood more about lines of sight than we did. I climbed over the gate and walked clockwise around two small stone circles before crossing the wet grass to a large cairn, facing east, and then turned and turned about to look at the faraway hills, one at each compass point, taking in the fresh air and open space. I stayed put, despite the chill.

It was after sunset when I reached the house. A man in an overcoat walked down the drive towards me. He made no remarks about why I was kicking stones on the road and not going in; he simply whispered a swift 'Hello, how are you?' as he passed me to get to his car. He would figure out who I was later. There were two derelict houses nearby, sinking into wet grassland without crops or live-stock. The whitethorn trees that were used to mark the boundaries of who owned what patch of ground were unremarkable until they blossomed in May. The place looked the same, no bigger, no smaller. The same.

A bungalow set behind a low garden wall with a small metal gate in the middle. The gate used to lead onto a stone path edged with flower beds. The path and the flower beds were gone. Poured concrete covered what was once a front garden and was now a car park. Every window was lit up. I imagined I was being watched where I stood and decided to make a move. Under its curved archway, the front door was open. A woman walked through it as I approached, backlit for a moment, then made her way to one of the cars, opened the boot and began lifting out biscuit tins and plastic tubs.

'Would you like some help?' I asked, with the distance of a car between us.

Easing her head out of the boot, she said, 'Who's that?'

'Hi, Mum.'

She straightened up. Two hands around her load.

'Mairéad.'

We stayed where we were. The last time we had been together was at the airport and I had barely said goodbye. The same gold necklace, a crescent moon, glinted on her neckline. Against a tawny-red, long, collarless knitted jacket made by my grandmother.

'Someone could have collected you, if we'd known when you were coming.'

'I went walking. To the old tombs.'

She adjusted the stack of food under one arm and shut the boot with the other.

'You were in hospital yourself this morning, Olwen said. I came here last night, without my address book, and then I couldn't remember anyone's number. Have you eaten? Are you cold?'

She took a step towards me, studying my face, and it

wasn't clear if she wanted to hug me or shake me. When I stepped back, she did the same, looking confused. I had hurt her feelings.

'I have to get these inside. Mammy is in the sitting-room, if you want to go in and see her? Your father is away on a job in Letterkenny. He'll be here in the morning.'

The coffin matched the length of the sitting-room window. There was a host of bodies crowded on and around the furniture, friends and neighbours leaning in to talk among themselves. A child holding an orange drink, perched on the arm of a chair just inside the door, turned to look at me. I put my bag under her seat and went directly to my grandmother. Laid out in blue tweed, eyes closed, mouth sealed. When I placed my hands over hers, they were the same size and shape and this unnerved me. Uncle Thomas stood at the foot of the coffin. Hair neatly side-parted, still a striking shade of red. In his good suit and polished shoes. Describing how she died to a small woman in an anorak.

'She woke up vomiting, with a terrible pain in her chest. She called me for help. And I called the ambulance straight away. "Stay with me," I told her. "Don't leave me." But she was gone. Massive heart attack, they said. Mammy could not have survived it.'

He didn't address me and I wondered if he was still in shock. His suit was possibly thirty years old, golden-brown with a subtle, darker stripe on the warp that you could only see up close. Bought for his sister's wedding and worn in every special-occasion photograph since then. I had forgotten it, but what else would Thomas wear to show respect? He must have brushed it and aired it and inspected the seams before putting it on over the milky coffee shades of his striped shirt and wide tie. It made him look vulnerable. The new boy, dressed for a big day ahead. The big day that was never his.

Olwen appeared and put an arm around me, stroking my sleeve before she spoke.

'Isn't she beautiful? Aunty Dervla said it's her favourite suit. Isn't it beautiful on her? And her best pin.'

We were the same height, my cousin and I, our shoulders pressing together. Snow-White and Rose-Red. There was a gold pin on a tweed lapel, leaf-shaped, with three seed pearls. Perfect for Yelena's travelling coat.

'Did my mum dress her?' I moved my hands to feel the material, examining the neat edging of a cuff.

'She did. Have you not seen Aunty Dervla?'

'Outside,' I said. I didn't have anything else to say about my mother. 'How is wee Amy? And you? Are you doing all right?'

'Dan put her to bed. I'd like a nap myself, to be honest,' Olwen's voice wavered, 'but I don't want to leave Granny on her own.' She brightened and said, 'Come out to the kitchen. You must be starving after your journey.'

My hand was holding the edge of the coffin and seemed to be keeping me there. 'I will in a minute,' I croaked, and Olwen hugged me closer before letting go and wrapping her oversized cardigan across her chest. The embalmer had applied peach-toned make-up to Granny Kate's skin. She looked smaller, without her breath. The energy that had floated about her yesterday was not gone. The dead weight we would bury; the lightness, the shape of her, would stay here, where she lived. My late grandmother. I placed my hands over hers once more and closed my eyes.

When I turned to face the room, a young man with a shaved head came towards me. Him. I was not ready for him. My cheeks were hot. Was he able to see I was blushing?

'You haven't forgotten me, have you?'

One hand in the pocket of his trousers, the other holding a bottle of beer. He smiled a tiny smile. The black suit was a particularly handsome one. Finely woven wool, single-button fastening, slimline leg. White shirt, black silk tie. I suppressed the desire to trace the jetted seams on the jacket, to pull it open and admire the satin lining. If I laid a hand on it, I would not be able to stop until it was next to my skin, protecting my back, soothing my shoulders. I was already staring for too long and raised my chin to snap out of it.

'When did you shave your hair?' There was a downy regrowth, like a fledgling.

'After Dad died. When I took over the business.'

His father, the butcher. Cold, hard work, he called it. And now Iggy was doing it. Without meaning to, I inspected his fingernails on the glass bottle. Clean as salt-scrubbed bone. A solid silver watch with a crimson face circling his wrist. We were seventeen when his dad got sick.

'Have you been here long?'

'No, no,' he said, shaking his head at the floor. He did that smile again and then said, 'I came straight after closing up. I heard your dad isn't coming until tomorrow.'

'Are you avoiding my father?' I asked.

'No.'

125

He looked closely at me and I needed a chair or a mantelpiece or something in my hands to grip. I had to rock on my heels and hold my stomach until the shaking in my knees eased off. His eyes, that I had told myself were too close together, were Arctic blue. A wolf in an overcrowded forest. His hair, for as long as I'd known him, had been long, often greasy, hiding his face. The principal of the boys' school used to draw a line in ball-point pen on his neck and instruct him to get it cut to there, but Iggy would rub it off. I suddenly hated everything I was wearing and wanted to tell him . . . what? Tell him what?

'How's London treating you? Olwen told me you got a start in a theatre.'

London. Where nobody swears with joy. Fluorescent lights on the Tube gouging at my eyeballs. Staring at the sky and wishing it were the sea. Two hours' journey to wherever I had to be. Constant fatigue. But. It was easy to go missing. A wonderful way to disappear.

'It's a great place for work,' I said.

Five men would be standing at dressingroom mirrors, getting ready for the evening show in a tempo of swift, definite movements. Snap, push, tighten. Slapping their hair into place and blurring the edges of the pan-stick. Pressing fake moustaches to binding tape. Pulling up a zipper that was concealed under cloth-covered buttons. Taking off a wedding ring. And Scott Gilbourne, catching my reflection, watching me watching him. You could see his eyelashes when he moved downstage, under the lights. How was I to defend myself against that? I had been struck dumb for most of the tech because of it. Ludicrous. Over a pretty face. Why were only good-looking people cast as lovers? It was a lie. Not all affairs took place over a lazy summer on a landlord's estate. Not all leading women were tragically beautiful. Not all leading men loved the sound of their own voice. Here was Iggy, who was not performing, who was not spoiled, who fed those around him, not just himself. Who had waited for me. That meant something.

'What happened to your eye?' he asked.

'Headbutted the show's producer yesterday. Ah, no, I banged it on a door by accident. How did you hear – about my grandmother?'

'Her neighbour is a customer. Wanted to remind me that we used to do deliveries out this way.'

'But you don't any more?'

'I would, if your grandmother had asked me.'

'Great news about the engagement, isn't it?' I had not noticed Olwen approaching until she stood between us with two plates of sandwiches. 'I have chicken and mayonnaise or ham and cheese. Take one, please. I can't go back into the kitchen until the plates are empty.'

The white bread looked like dried wallpaper paste and I imagined the fillings congealing inside my colon and arteries. I wasn't going to touch the things.

'Who got engaged?' I asked her, averting my nose from the food.

'I'm engaged,' Iggy said.

I should not have laughed. That was inappropriate. He shifted away from me and I put my arm out to halt him, then pulled it back.

'It's great, isn't it?' Olwen repeated, with too much enthusiasm. There were tears in her eyes as she closed

127

them over. 'Granny loved weddings. The hats! She had beautiful taste in hats.'

The only hats of hers I remembered were ones she had knitted. I turned away from Olwen to lie to Iggy's face.

'Congratulations. Delighted for you. Anyone I know?' I didn't want to give a shit who it was. I wanted to launch myself in a flaming hot-air balloon and disappear from the planet forever.

'I dunno. Sylvia O'Grady? From Ballyshannon? She's a teacher. Went to college in Dublin.'

I made a show of mentally scanning my awareness of a Sylvia. O'Grady. From Ballyshannon. What I was remembering was the first time I had sex with Iggy. The leathery sound of skin on skin, his hips butting against mine. I could not relax. He stopped. It only happened a few times afterwards because I couldn't let go of the tension in my body. Even so, a rumour started and spread until a fine, upstanding moral guardian bent his breast and ran to tell my father a half-story. I had to deal with my dad threatening to shoot the fella that had touched me. Or me, if I didn't give him a name, as if nothing had changed since daughters were property and another man had stolen his. Running to the beach on my own and staying there long after dark. The bruise around my eye hurt. It was an impossible riddle, being female.

'Will you take a sandwich, please?' Olwen begged.

'Doesn't ring a bell,' I said, shaking my head at the two of them and holding my lips in a tight grimace.

'We haven't set a date yet, but we will. Still sort of getting our heads around it,' he said.

Olwen went over to a side table crammed with dirty cups and glasses. She lowered the plate of chicken sandwiches on top of them, capped it with the cheese and ham, and walked outside. I made a move to follow her, but Iggy touched my elbow. A man sitting on a footstool began to sing.

'Met anyone famous? In the theatre?' Iggy asked.

He could not know how bored I was of the need for 'anyone famous'. Never asked about my work, only about bloody actors.

'I washed Harry Adley's underpants. Y-fronts, if you want to know.'

Watching the information move across his face, I realised I was being selfish. He was doing his best to keep up the conversation.

'Right, I'll bear it in mind. He was on *Parkinson*, for some big film, wasn't he? What's he like, in real life?'

'He's a pervert,' I said.

The drop of his features, pulling his head away and retreating. They wanted me to tell them about serenades through dressingroom walls, the generous tips left to the lowest-paid among us, the colour-blind stars who couldn't use the green-red lighting cues and were so humble about it; yes, they did say 'darling' because they didn't know your name. 'If you meet an actor,' I told people, 'be sure to ask them how they remember their lines. They love answering that question.'

My mother's first cousin had picked up the plates of squashed sandwiches and was making her way over to us. I wasn't going to let her turn me into a hostess.

'Thanks for coming, Iggy,' I mumbled, turning to leave the room.

'I'm sorry for your trouble,' he said, meaning my dead grandmother.

'And congratulations, I . . . I'm very . . . I—' The man was singing 'The Last Rose of Summer' as my feet crossed the threshold. I had not allowed myself to think of Iggy for so long. Had his eyes always been that blue?

Outside, there was a sharp scent of pine from a set of potted trees. Granny Kate's portable Christmas props. I wandered past the gable wall and on to the back of the house, searching for Olwen.

'Mairéad, come over here.'

It wasn't Olwen, it was her mother, Veronica, wearing what looked like a military greatcoat and sitting on the garden seat my grandmother repainted with white gloss each summer. Veronica could have been an army general, avoiding the civilians inside, waiting for the inevitable return to war.

'It's dry,' she said, indicating the space beside her with a tip of her glass. The cast iron was cold under my bum. Veronica seemed unable to let go of the tumbler in her hand. Scanning my face from left to right, she said, 'The state of you. What did you do to yourself?'

I cleared my throat and felt my voice returning. 'Not as bad as it looks, Aunty Vee. You should see the other fella.'

A nudge from her elbow. 'Do you want the end of this? There's only a finger left. Whiskey. Medicinal.'

'No, thanks,' I said. It smelled like warm petrol.

'Did anyone tell you the funeral is on Monday morning, ten o'clock?'

'Monday? Not tomorrow?'

'Mairéad, love, there's nothing available tomorrow.' Her relaxed tone didn't help.

'But I have to get back to work.' How would I make it back for the evening show on Monday? I thought I'd be in London by then. Well, I thought wrong, didn't I? Margaret might have replaced me already. As soon as I decided to come here, she would have crossed me off the roster.

Veronica didn't move, except to close her eyes. 'I am going to put that comment down to shock, Mairéad. My mother has just died. Maybe you could think about that?'

'And forget about my little dressing-up job, forget about keeping my promises?' I said sharply, then wanted to unsay it immediately. There was no way she would understand why I felt like I had abandoned my fellow soldiers at the front. No one else in this house thought about a distant world going on without me. 'That came out wrong,' I said. 'I'm sorry. I'm tired.' There would be other jobs. Had I not just told Iggy London was a great place for work? 'Funeral on Monday, of course. What do you need me to do?'

Veronica opened her eyes and spoke carefully, controlling her temper. 'For tonight, I've said this to Olwen and I'm telling you now, there is no need for the who-can-stay-awake-the-longest competition. Get some rest. We'll need you to help with the visitors tomorrow.' She paused. 'Although, with that face, we might keep you behind the scenes.'

'The way I like it,' I said, grateful for her patience.

Drinking back the dregs of her glass, she set it down on the ground. 'When you were a wee girl, you used to bring flowers to your granny. Little bunches of dandelions, or daisies and clover. Weeds, in other words. But I liked that you did it. You're a kind person, Mairéad. Don't lose sight of yourself.'

Veronica was more forgiving than her sister. 'Do you remember taking us on long walks when I was the same wee girl? To show us old forts and passage graves.'

'They weren't long enough. I was trying to tire you out.' She raised her arm over my head, took hold of my shoulder and brought me closer to her. 'Or maybe I just wanted to get out of the house.'

The heavy wool of her coat was as warm as a blanket and I felt my muscles relaxing, letting go of the awful day, the overwhelming sadness. A blackbird was lilting in the branches of a birch tree.

'If I'm kind, Aunty Vee, I must have learned it from you.'

'Go to the kitchen.' She squeezed my arm for emphasis. 'Eat something, drink something, say goodnight to Mam and then find a place to sleep. We'll need each other to get through this, believe me.'

The crowd had thinned inside the house; no one else was in the kitchen. I poured a glass of cold water from the tap and put a slice of apple tart on a porcelain plate. They had taken out the good china. There was a place to sit at the table, where I raised a forkful of pastry and spiced filling to my mouth, and then lowered it. I wasn't being obstinate, I genuinely had no appetite. I put the broken bits of tart into the scrap bucket for Rex, Thomas's black Labrador, and rinsed off the plate.

He sent me a Valentine's card once. I had forgotten that. I had completely forgotten that. The first time Iggy kissed me, we were drinking in the football stands at the back of his school. A group of us. Without any warning, he had grabbed me and put me in a headlock, crushing my nose against his neck as we both folded over. I was barely able to breathe or to move my face as he kissed one half of my mouth. I thought he was being clumsy and would make a joke about it, so I waited and heard him take a breath. Then he did it again, slowly. There was a gentle pressure from his fingertips on my chin. His mouth. Inviting me forwards and in, to him. I wanted to open my eyes and search for a sign he wasn't serious and I wanted to keep my eyes closed to enjoy the feeling. Someone wolf-whistled and he broke off, laughing, and let me go.

They were singing 'Peggy Gordon' in the front room. With little capacity to speak or to think clearly, I went in and kissed my grandmother goodnight on her forehead. I found my mother in her mother's bed, lying on one side, cradling her face in her hands. I stood in the doorway and she gestured for me to lie down beside her. At some stage, we both fell asleep.

Easter Sunday, 31 March 2002

My mother woke first, before dawn. Her soft weeping woke me. She had turned away, so I rested my hand on her upper spine, to let her know I was here, I came back. Someone had put an extra blanket over us during the night and our breaths synchronised under its warmth.

'The clocks have gone forward an hour,' she told the wall. 'It's summertime.'

She got up and put on my grandmother's dressing-gown and her own slip-on shoes before leaving the room. I thought my body might fall back to sleep. As the sun rose and the light took over, I gave up on that thought.

Thomas was minding the coffin when I went into the sitting-room, head bent over his rosary beads. His 1970s wide-collared Aran cardigan was pristine. Jacqui would love it. My mother was hand-stitching a hem on someone's funeral trousers. I sat on the armrest of the two-seater couch and watched as she reeled out a line of thread from the small spool in her lap and snapped it off with her fingers, grimacing as she pulled. She wet the thread between her lips and reloaded the needle. It was seven-thirty on a Sunday morning but it felt like the middle of the night. I was impressed with how awake they both were, how alert.

'Will you think about reading a prayer of the faithful at the Mass tomorrow, Mairéad?' she asked me.

'Would you like me to do that?' I pointed at the trousers. 'Hand them over to me and I'll finish it.'

'Your stitches are not as neat as mine,' she said, smiling at her work.

Thomas paused, a bead between his finger and thumb. 'You have the gift,' he said to his sister and gave a short puff through his nostrils. She had a mathematical mind and had taught herself to stitch fluently. At least teach the child to sew on the machine, was my grandmother's plea, because my mother had one. No one will pay you properly for your labour, was the reason why not. Unless you were male. That was high-and-mighty talk from someone with a daughter who didn't have a nice dress to wear on Sundays. And off they would go.

'One day, I'll take a lesson from you,' I said to her. 'One day, when you're not too busy.'

'That would be lovely,' she replied, checking the hem was even all the way round.

I went into the empty kitchen, filled the kettle, then sat and rested my head on my folded arms, face-down on the table.

'Sitting on your backside as usual, Mairéad?' He filled the frame of the open back door, holding a wide cardboard box branded with the logo of a meat company.

'I'm pretending to be a man,' I said, resuming my go-to-sleep pose as water came to the boil.

'What happened to your eye?' He stood beside me and

lifted me by the jaw, leaning in to examine the bruise. The box of food was left on top of the electric rings on the cooker.

'Walked into a door, Dad. A cheap kitchen cupboard, knocked it off its hinges.'

'I feel sorry for the door.' He tilted my head from side to side and then pressed my shoulders together, like an accordion player. 'Get up and get your father a cup of tea, good girl. I'm parched.' His attention moved to the current state of the room as he continued talking. 'I remember when my own mother died, I didn't leave the kitchen for three days straight, making tea and buttering bread. But this is not my house.' He pointed to his gift: the makings of a fry to feed the five thousand. 'Put the lot on. They'll eat it.'

My father was currently a delivery driver and liked to arrive bearing gifts of pork products or frozen foods. He had also been, in no particular order, a wedding singer, a potato picker, a navvy, a painter, a travelling salesman of Country and Western CDs and a bus conductor. He thought he would inherit and expand his family farm. It went to the bank instead.

Thomas must have heard him booming from the other room.

'Felim Sweeney,' he said, coming in to marvel at his girth.

My father put one hand over his heart and bowed his head. 'I'm sorry for your trouble, Thomas, it's a terrible blow for you.'

'It is.' Thomas put his rosary in a cardigan pocket and stood with his arms dangling by his sides.

'Will you have a rasher?' my father asked, gripping the back of my chair and pitching me out of it.

137

'I will, aye, surely, Felim.' Thomas, glowing with relief at somebody taking charge, sat down at the table. My father took the chair I had vacated.

'Mairéad. Bail ó Dhia ar an obair.' Meaning, Get to work, daughter, while I comfort the bereaved. The slightest narrowing of my eyes and a tightening of my lips was all I could manage by way of disobedience. Challenge him now and he would pull down the sky. I could not comfort Thomas. A grill and a frying pan, at least, would expect no conversation from me. I opened the cardboard box.

'Who are the grapefruits for?' Two of them, inside a brown bag.

'Pass one over to me. And a small sharp knife,' he said.

'Are you still off the cigarettes?' Thomas asked him.

'I am. Three years. Four, next month.'

Although my back was turned to him, I could sense the disappointment on Thomas's face. He was almost as desperate for a smoke as he was for sympathetic male company. I pictured Margaret at her desk, rolling, not tapping, the ash from her cigarette. Swirling it in a crystal ashtray.

'Me too,' he said. 'Still off them, I mean.'

Only when his sisters were watching, or when he had no one, no man, to stand by him. I was at it already. Typecasting. Peddling family propaganda that we were only one thing: Thomas was too sensitive, my mother was cold, my father was old-fashioned and I was moody. What would it take to undo it, to bring home the news that the authorities were wrong?

'Heart attack, wasn't it?'

Thomas opened his mouth to retell the story, but got nowhere.

'I mind the last time I saw your mother, God bless her. She had that vegetable patch cleared and ready to go with new seeds. There was no one to match her, she could coax gold from straw. May she rest in peace, Thomas, she certainly earned it.' Death was not to be shied away from. Felim had come to bring it out into the light like a newborn calf, the mess and the pain and the extraordinary ordinariness of it. 'Remember Mrs O'Neill?' he said. 'You do, you do, you do. Husband and brother-in-law on the same trawler. Drowned. Five years before they found any remains. I said to her, at the graveside, I said, "You have him home at last, Mrs O'Neill." "I know where he is now," she said back to me. "I know where he is."'

'She did,' Thomas said gently as I put out a pot of tea, 'the poor woman.'

The smell of the fry brought Veronica and her husband, Hugh, to the kitchen, followed by Olwen, her husband and her daughter; everyone save my mother, who was sitting with the coffin, Veronica said. She would not come into the room with my father there.

My father slapped his thigh at the sight of Olwen's daughter. 'Amy Sheehy, you're growing like a weed! What are they feeding you?' and the child hesitated to take the fork her mother was handing her. 'I'm, I'm four, five, seven, nine,' she said, holding up all her fingers, 'I'm nine.'

'She's three, Uncle Felim,' Olwen said, 'and she'll bite your leg if you forget to give her breakfast, won't she, Dan?' Olwen's husband raised his palms and said it was just the once and by Jesus he'd not repeat that mistake.

As soon as I added cooked food to the serving dishes in the middle of the table, it disappeared. Told you so, my father winked, barely stopping for breath in his monologue about my grandmother. Veronica appeared next to me as I cut open the last packet of sausages and handed over an empty plate.

'Make one up for your mother, before it's all gone,' she whispered. She took my place at the pan and I arranged some bread, two eggs and two sausages on the plate and began to make my way to the other room.

'Wait a minute.' My father presented me with a cereal bowl into which he had cut a grapefruit into bite-size pieces and spiked one of the pieces with a small fork. 'Get a tray and take this to your mother with a cup of tea,' he said.

Mum shook her head at the offering. 'The tea will do me. You can take away the rest.' Because the rest had been touched by fat. Was there one part of her body she found no fault with? Her inner ear maybe. Her duodenum.

'All right,' I said, but I left the cut grapefruit behind. When I returned to the kitchen with the rejected breakfast, I felt pity for it. 'There is nothing wrong with you,' I said to the eggs, in my head. 'I won't let you go to waste.' The kitchen surfaces were overflowing with the workings of food. Even the trestle table that had been brought in to make more space was covered in tubs and boxes, but there was a spot at the end of the counter, away from the toaster and kettle, where I could lean without knocking into a tower of plastic or tin foil. I stood there, eating with one hand, savouring each mouthful of salted butter on soda bread.

'It's Easter Sunday. Isn't anyone going to Mass?' Thomas asked. The first to finish, he had slotted his knife into his fork and positioned them at six o'clock on his plate. He had been waiting for the others to stop eating, but they did not have his moderate appetite.

'I'll take you, if you want,' Hugh said, putting one more load into his mouth before pushing the rest away from him. He looked at Thomas with his arms folded while Dan looked across at Hugh. They both want to take him, I thought, and it was a mean thought, but they won't lift a finger to clear the table.

Veronica turned off the cooker and said she didn't see how we could go. We needed to get things ready. People would be arriving soon.

'But it's Easter,' Thomas persisted.

'You can go to Mass every day for the next year after tomorrow, Thomas,' Veronica said, 'when we're not burying our mother.'

The sight of the grease congealing on the dishes did not seem to prompt anyone else into action. I lifted the kettle to check how much hot water was left. Enough to make a start on the washing-up. Olwen said she would get herself and Amy dressed. From his seat at the table, my father asked Thomas if he wanted to tidy up outside, clear away any cigarette butts or empty glasses, that type of thing.

'Mairéad,' he ordered, 'leave that. Go and get ready.'

I shook the suds from my hands and turned around. 'Are you going to finish it?' I asked.

'Yes. If you'll get out of the way. Hugh and Dan can help me. Don't worry, there'll be plenty more. And when you come back, we'll start buttering bread.'

141

'Fine by me,' I said. I was pleased to see him put the others to work. When I walked through the front room, Thomas was back at his mother's side.

'Dervla wants me to stay here,' he said.

I found her in Granny Kate's room, sitting on the edge of the bed, this time in a long-sleeved dress with a high collar and a belted waist. It wasn't black; it was dark green.

'You look nice,' I told her. 'Granny always wanted us to look nice.'

'And to sit decent,' she said, hands in her lap.

'I left my blacks at the theatre. I feel stupid now.'

My mother began lacing up a pair of soft leather brogues that suited her outfit. 'It isn't the 1950s, Mairéad. You don't have to wear black.'

But I wanted to wear black, not a worsted purple polo neck and navy-blue jeans. I looked fucking awful.

Veronica welcomed the guests and led them to the front room to pay their last respects to my grandmother's body with a short prayer, a sign of the cross, a kiss on her forehead. They came all day: sisters-in-law, first cousins, first cousins once removed, second cousins, neighbours, friends, family from the North with their Portrush accents that were louder and faster than any other, talking across each other. Thomas was once again standing in his suit at the foot of the coffin, shaking hands with each newcomer and repeating how his mother had died: 'She woke up vomiting, with a terrible pain in her chest—'

The front room filled like a spring tide. The kitchen, the hallway and the porch were jammed with bodies, forcing people to move outside to talk, despite the rain.

My clothes were too warm and too tight. Women would put their hand on my arm and ask me if I wanted a break from the washing-up? I'd say, 'No, thank you.' If they pressured me, I'd whisper that I didn't want to keep explaining what had happened to my face. Talking out loud would make my stomach cramp and my eyes water, and they'd say, 'All right, if you're sure,' and leave me be. One of them asked me if I knew the Queen Mother over in England had died on the same day as Kate.

A visitor brought a casserole in a slow cooker and plugged it in beside the bread bin. Brack and fruit cake were cut into fingers and sent around. Cheesecakes were abandoned for lack of forks and side plates to eat them. My father set Hugh and Dan on a carousel of platters of sandwiches, buttered scones, fairy cakes, jam tarts and ginger biscuits, pausing frequently for the serious business of socialising with a familiar face. If he caught my eye, he would introduce me to a stranger as 'You do know them. You do, you do, you do', smothering the possibility that I did not recognise the multiple connections between us. A husband and wife had driven a long distance for the event and my father instructed me to organise a large plate and two freshly washed teacups for them.

'You made the sandwiches yourself, Felim, I can tell,' the woman said. 'Do you want to know how I know?' She was standing between the two men, holding the plate, with her cup in the other hand. It was her husband who was eating the sandwich.

'They're not soggy. The ones you buy nowadays, they must think we're eejits, pumping the meat full of water to bump up the weight. Well, I can tell when it's proper meat. You rarely get it. Only in the upmarket establishments.'

'Only for our upmarket guests, madam!' My father made an elaborate bow to her and rose up taller than he had been, boosted by the praise. Her smile came after his and I was back in the theatre, stuck in a crowd of people who were tiptoeing around one man. The realisation sickened me. Heaven forbid we should upset Felim and make him lose his temper. How many times had I pandered to him like this? I looked at that big red face and wanted to dump a bowl of trifle over it to show I was not taken in by his act. That would change the mood. I didn't do it, but I enjoyed the thought for a second before I went back to my station. Through the window over the sink, I saw my mother in the back garden, sitting on the bench under an umbrella, holding a cigarette and not smoking it.

There was a lull in the parade of visitors after seven o'clock.

'We put it in the funeral notice.' Veronica stacked one more pile of dirty dishes on the table. '*House private after 7 p.m.* Let them go home and have their dinner.' Which meant the pains in my stomach were hunger pangs.

'Come in to the front room with us.' She pointed to the dishes. 'Leave those for now.'

'I'll follow you in,' I said.

When I was alone, I took a clean bowl, filled it with casserole and sat down with two slices of bread and the butter dish. Olwen wandered in from the garden, holding Amy against her chest.

'She puked up a bellyful of cake and fizzy drinks outside and the dog is eating it,' Olwen said. 'Dan and Hugh went off to the pub with the Portrush gang and we're going to sit quietly in here, aren't we, dotey?' Olwen put her hand on Amy's back and mouthed 'Bedtime' to me over her head as she lowered herself into Grandad's old chair, kissing her child's crown and rocking her as she turned to look out of the window. The sunset was not spectacular, there were more clouds than sky, but the changing light was calming. Yelena was right. You should trust people.

'Olwen,' I was feeling the benefit of the warm meal, 'thanks for trying to get through to me, in London, about Granny.'

'That was Mum. I did have a moment of panic, I don't mind telling you, after your boss — Mum said she was very curt — told us you were not at work.'

'Did you think I might have had a heart attack as well?'

'I thought,' Olwen put her hands over Amy's ears and dropped her voice, 'that you were lying dead on the street, with millions of people stepping over your body, and we'd never find you again.' She eased back into the chair and gave me a wink.

'Well, the Piccadilly murders only happen on a new moon, you see.' I spoke softly in turn, to avoid rousing Amy. 'Once the moon changes,' a connecting thought occurred to me, 'it's safe to be out after dark.' My day-long hunger pangs were period cramps.

Olwen's lips widened and tightened in what might have been an attempt to smile or to hold back tears. She probably had not sat down all day.

'There's plenty of casserole left. Will I fix you a bowl?'

She shook her head and then bent over Amy's face. 'Almost there. Still fighting it, but we're almost there.'

145

Raising her eyes to me, she whispered, 'No one can die . . .'

'Until the tide goes out,' I replied.

'Poor Granny Kate. I don't know if the tide was in or out when she went.'

'Do you remember one time, we were here on our summer holidays, watching a film with Granny, something American, when one of the characters asked another if they were a virgin? What did I do but turn around and ask, "What's a virgin?" and she said, "I'll tell you later," but then you piped up with the answer.'

'Did I? Oh, no, what did I say?' Olwen put her fingers to her lips.

'"A virgin," you told me, "is the highest rank for a saint, next only to God. But you have to be dead before you can become one."'

'Is that what I told you?'

'That, or something like it. We were very pious. I can't remember what Granny said, except she didn't contradict you.'

'I'm so glad you're here. No one else would indulge me and my fairy tales.'

'Of the many incredible things that happened before I was born? You had a tail. You taught a horse to speak. You lived in New York and met Madonna. You had a tame pet chicken.'

'The pet chicken was true! I used to put a soft belt around her neck and take her for a walk.'

I ran my spoon around the inside of the bowl, telling myself I had had enough. 'Do you know her, Sylvia O'Grady?'

'Who?'

'Iggy Keogh's fiancée.'

'No, never met her. It's nice you stayed friends. Didn't he play the drums in Brian's band for a while?'

'Two very different groups. Iggy's band was good. Relatively.' Another item that broke up when he finished school. We weren't friends. I didn't know how to explain it to Olwen. I took one more mouthful of bread.

'Mother of God, the noise that used to come out of our garage. They were dire, but you can't say that to Brian. Touchy subject.'

'Is he on a flight?'

'Landed. Mum told him to go to our house and get some sleep, be ready for the funeral tomorrow. What do you think will happen to this place, without Granny?' Olwen cast a long look around the kitchen, as if she were watching our childhood summers and Christmases together. When I was small, I used to ask when my mum was coming to collect me. Granny would tell me she'd come as soon as she'd finished work. Wasn't I happy with her in the meantime? Then she'd give me a job or a treat and I'd stop asking. If I had felt lonesome, or stranded, it was unintentional. My grandmother was glad to have me.

'Remember a few years ago, when Uncle Thomas got the dog and he said that's why he had to leave his flat in Carrick? Do you think he just wanted to be here, at home?'

'Are you getting a dog, Mairéad?'

The laugh burst out of me and I had to put both hands over my mouth and shake my head.

Olwen cuddled her daughter tighter and made sounds that were somewhere between laughing and shushing.

147

'I think he wanted to mind Granny. Same as the rest of us. You know I hated knitting? And baking? Never in a million years was I going to finish that terrible scarf, but I didn't want to upset her by telling her.'

Our relationships with our grandmother were as different as our mothers. Mine had mocked Granny Kate for constantly training us to be obedient little housewives. Veronica and Thomas had rounded on her at the time, and I had agreed with them. No child should be an only child. This was something my grandmother repeated to my mother in front of me. 'You want to keep me locked indoors,' was her response. I wanted a sibling and a happier mother.

'London is doing me good. The scale of it, the pulse, even the way people dress. It makes me want to keep moving, to go further than anyone expected.' I surprised myself as I spoke and also believed it was true. 'It'll be a while before I get a dog.'

We regarded each other across the table, sharing an easy peacefulness. Amy had moved her thumb into her mouth and Olwen lifted it out again. 'I might put her down before Uncle Felim starts asking me where Dan and Hugh disappeared to.' She caught my eye. 'No offence, Mairéad, but he is loud.'

'He is a foghorn. Get out while you can.'

'I'll probably fall asleep with her. The long day is catching up with me.'

'Night, night, Amy,' I said as Olwen rose from her seat.

'Bye-bye,' she said softly, waving her baby fingers a fraction, her head heavy with drowsiness.

After they had gone, the plates of sweet stuff in the room were all I could think about, like money in my pocket I had to spend. Staying in the kitchen on my own meant I would be unable to stop eating until I also ended up outside, puking in front of the dog. Going into the sitting-room meant I would have to talk. If I had two rooms to live in, I would spend my days believing I should be in the other one.

The door between the kitchen and the sitting-room closed with a pleasing snap. A solid barrier between me and the tables full of food. Or not so solid. With my backside pushing against it, the plywood felt as brittle as honeycomb.

Four heads turned in my direction. Dervla and Veronica on either side of the fire, Thomas beside the coffin. My father was sitting to my left, rubbing his neck and smiling at me.

'Here comes Yves Saint Laurent, looking for the good scissors. Half-day for you, is it, Yves? Time to put away the frocks?'

'Even God took a break to loosen Her girdle,' I said.

There was a flicker of confusion across his face and then he broke into a loud laugh. Very loud. Whiskey. The heaviness that came over me started at the corners of my eyes and continued down my throat like cod liver oil. I had walked into the bull's field. If he was drinking, he would make sure the focus was on his humour, not mine.

'God's girdle! The Lord save us. There's a place here for you. Sit down with your family.' He patted the empty chair beside him, watching me as he did so.

It was restful, leaning against the door, and I wanted to close my eyes and sink into sleep. When I didn't move, he stopped smiling.

'Sit down,' he repeated.

Nobody else spoke. I used my hands to press myself up and went over to the chair. There were crumbs on the seat. Before I had finished swiping them off, the conversation began again.

'Did you see Evelyn MacCready?' Thomas moved his thumbs continuously, one over the other. He was talking quickly, addressing my father. 'She said it's been twenty years since her husband died. Twenty years. For the first year – she held my hands when she said this, so sincere, so elegant – she had to keep telling herself he was dead. Whenever she heard wellingtons being scraped at the door, she said she forgot what had happened and was convinced he would walk in. "I had to keep saying it out loud," that's what she told me. "He's gone. He's gone and he's not coming back."'

'She's put on a sight of weight,' my father declared. His cerise tie followed the S-curve of his gut, its wide tip tucked into the waistband, concealing where the lower buttons on his shirt undoubtedly gaped with the strain.

'But she has beautiful hair.' Thomas beseeched approval from his brother-in-law. 'She was awfully good to us after Daddy passed away. Some of the neighbours were on at Mammy to sell this place, move into town. "But what would you do in town?" Evelyn said to her.'

'Evelyn was right,' Veronica said. 'They thought they'd take advantage, get the farm for a song. Larry Redihan arrived in his clapped-out Mercedes, waving some ridiculous piece of paper, and tried to bully her into signing it over to him. "Let the geese out," Mammy said, "if he ever darkens our door again."'

'Did she?' Thomas bit his lip and smiled across at his

sister. 'I never knew that. Wasn't she remarkable?' He paused, considering something. 'I remember her talking to Daddy after he died. When she'd say, "Amn't I right, Tom? Wouldn't you agree with me?" I thought she could see his ghost.'

'She did that when she wanted you to feel guilty,' my mother said.

'She wanted things done properly, the way they should be,' Thomas replied. 'Victor Casey had my head turned about going to New York to work for Pan Am. Can you imagine? School first, she insisted. Well, Victor couldn't wait and he took the boat. He's trying to become a pilot yet, as far as I know. I got my exams and my sales apprenticeship in Harrison's. People will always need shoes.'

There was a sharp pinch in my lower back. Inflammation. I needed to lie flat with my knees bent, or not sit on a chair.

'Your face looks worse today,' my mother said, examining me from her armchair. 'Did you put anything over that eye?'

'I didn't. Would there be a bag of peas in the freezer?' It was unlikely I'd find peas in Granny Kate's freezer. Ice cream, maybe, but probably not packets of frozen vegetables, not when she had a garden full of her own greens. It was also too late to start pressing cold things to my face. It would do nothing for the bruising.

'I meant make-up. Have you got some for tomorrow?' she asked.

'No.' I pushed down on my pelvis and cocked my legs out in front of me, separating my feet widely to examine my swollen ankles.

'Mairéad, in the name of decency, you can't sit like

that.' It was the first time since I'd arrived that Thomas had made eye contact with me. 'Close your legs. What would your granny say if she saw you?'

He frowned slightly and crossed his own legs. Did he expect me to model him? The rush of anger that filled my throat was uncontrollable. Jacqui would have pushed her thighs further apart with her hands. Philippa would have piled a bloody litter of archaic insults in the centre of the tufted carpet: 'Cover up my kiln hole, my placket, my no-thing, is it?'

'Granny is dead.' I levelled my gaze at Thomas, despising his sanctimony. 'She has nothing more to say.' A stinging rash rising from my chest to my face cut me off. I hated blushing. Its burning heat stopped my tongue when I wanted to keep going. *So keep going.* I heard the thought like a prompt, from beside myself. Look at him. He was not conceived by the power of the Holy Spirit, he was made from as much sweat and labour as everyone else.

'You went in and came out of your mother the same way as the rest of us, Thomas. It's a wonder you are so terrified of the equipment.'

The silence that followed was dreadful. It bulged against the four walls and filled my ears like a drop in air pressure. I had strayed too far, distracted by a flash of colour, and made myself the target. Nothing grew except the silence. Thomas looked at me as blankly as my grandparents in their wedding photograph, as though I were a distant, unrecognisable object. He pressed one hand to his heart and made a brief 'Halt' sign with the other, in case I had any notion of approaching him while he regained his composure.

A sudden movement beside me took my attention from

my uncle. Reflexively, I grabbed the hand raised to hit me. Wide awake again with rage, I leaned out and wrestled my father's arm back to his body, crushing his wrist with my ironing muscles. I wanted to break it. With his chin pushed inwards and his round face, he resembled a gigantic, belligerent bullfinch. He could fuck off and die himself if he thought he was going to hold me hostage.

'Give it over, Mairéad. Did you think I was going to slap you?' He shook off my hold and went back to rubbing his neck. The shock of misreading him was the same as tripping over in public and landing face-down in the muck. My mother snorted. There was nothing to do except look foolish. I crossed my ankles and tucked my legs under the chair.

'Even if you did deserve it,' he muttered.

'Stop,' Veronica said.

His cheeks inflated with wind from his guts and he puffed it out with a sigh. The smell was acidic. He had meant to hit me, hadn't he? It was imprinted on him: strike first and don't let up. The amount of times in the past when he had slapped me and then automatically put his hand over my mouth. The scratch of the cracked skin on his finger and thumb tips, the moisture from my breath collecting on his palm and my chin. It was impossible to wriggle out of his grip. I used to try to nip at his flesh with my front teeth, but that had only made it worse.

He swung his jaw from side to side. 'We had a bradach cow growing up. When I tried to milk her, she lashed me around the head with her tail. I brought her to the fair and had to bring her all the way home again. No one wanted the bad-mannered creature.'

'Felim, that's enough.' Veronica sounded restrained, not wanting to fight.

'Dehorned nowadays, of course. You wouldn't put up with it.' He had clearly not said enough. 'Your mother could put manners on a bad-tempered cow, Veronica. She knew how to handle them.'

The confusion I had felt when I was a child returned, in miniature, like a broken toy. The confusion, but not the fear. The terror of him hitting me again was gone. I knew what was coming when he declared his intention to 'put manners on me'. It was his regular practice to show me who was the boss. When he went too far, I was to blame for bringing it on. It wasn't enough for him to win; he had to make sure you knew you had lost.

'Aye, Mammy understood them,' Veronica replied. 'Traded them by herself. They used to say, do you remember this, Dervla? They used to say she was as good as a man.'

'Silence is not peace,' I said, unrushed. 'A dog is silent before it bites you.' I did not shrink inwards, I did not hold myself rigid. I was thinking about how he used to reappear in a doorway afterwards, flexing a pound note, crouching down to my child height to declare that we were going to the shop. 'Pick something your mother wouldn't let you have.' Then he would use his loudest voice to buy two packets of the same cheap chocolate or sticky sweets: one for him, one for me. We would sit on the windowsill outside to chew. 'Don't tell her about this,' he'd say, filled to the brim with his great idea. 'She doesn't understand how to enjoy life.' The grand gesture did him no favours. It didn't erase the slap.

'I miss the cows.' Thomas reached out to hold the edge of the coffin. 'But I do not miss the morning milking. The thought of going back to that—' He held his eyelids shut for a second and turned down the corners of his mouth. 'No,' he said, 'I am not a morning person.'

Granny used to make rugs as a way of expressing her anger, or so I believed. I remembered her rapidly, force-fully, pulling strands of wool through the mesh backing with gritted teeth, muttering curses she wouldn't say aloud. Ignoring what I said. They had sent me out into the world to be a bystander.

Thomas twisted his upper body slightly, towards the window. 'I used to like feeding the calves. I knew where they would end up, of course I did, but.' His eyelids flickered and he waved the air with his free hand, conducting something, outside in the darkness, close to the warm belly of an animal. He was pale and thin-lipped and I was sorry for being so brutal with him. I wondered if he noticed how my hands were the same as his mother's and if that was why he couldn't look at me. His poor dog was outside and I hoped it had gone up to the barn. It might have helped to have its friendly face among us.

'The times we spent nursing a sick calf.' Veronica's eyes were half-closed as she spoke. 'Dozing beside them on the hay.'

'There is nothing sweeter than the smell of hay,' my father said, pushing back any potential argument with an outswing of his arm.

The smell of hay made me gag. I'd have to stand upwind, especially if it was damp. Sonya spent the first two acts of *Uncle Vanya* worrying about the hay. No one else gave a shit if it was saved or not. She was left to solve the problem on her own.

'And the barley. You'd drink in the smell of barley. Going out to mow a field at first light, I'd have that scythe sharpened like a, a—' He was sharpening the curve of an imaginary blade on a whetstone when he froze for a second with his mouth open. Then he faced me, thumping the side of his chair.

'It is a sin to speak ill of the dead!'

He could not resist it. He had to correct my mouth with his fist.

'After all your grandmother did for you, Mairéad, for anyone to disrespect her, let alone her own granddaughter, I am ashamed of you. Your turn will come, don't think it won't, and what will people say about you?'

He sat back and crossed his thick forearms. A large, art-deco mirror hung from a chain above the tiled fireplace, pitched at an angle into the room. I saw his reflection between the tarnished corners. You massive ham, I thought. He was watching the others, waiting for their reaction. Below the mirror, the turf in the grate was stacked like a dolmen. It smouldered with no flame, releasing fragments of ash and the smell of smoked honey. If he was putting that much effort into his indignation, it had to be for his own sake. To control what was said and not said about him after he died.

'Why don't you write it down?' It was easier to talk to the mirror, but I turned directly to him, to avoid any misunderstanding. 'Write down what I'm not allowed to mention at a wake. You'd enjoy that, making a list of injunctions. See if it will stop me from saying what I think.' There was a pleasant dropping away of the rage I had felt earlier. I was balanced. Ready to undo an ugly fastening for good. 'You're ashamed of me? What you mean is, you want to wallop me but there are too many people watching.'

'Is this how they behave over in London?' Thomas kept his hand on the coffin and spoke to the floor. 'That she may learn to drop that language into the sea before she comes home again.'

'Thomas,' Veronica said, 'don't get involved, for Christ's sake.'

'It doesn't suit you,' my father sighed, 'trying to be smart with me.' He tucked his neck into his chin once more and gazed down the length of his body. 'By the time I was your age, Mairéad, I had buried both of my parents. Whatever I have, whatever I am, it came from them. Broke their own backs to build us a better future. There's no machine in the world could work as hard as they did.' Keeping his head down, he tilted his face slightly to one side and swivelled his eyeballs towards me. 'Why do you only want to knock things down? Any fool can do that. Why don't you try to build something? You'll get much further with generosity than bitterness.' He sat up and cupped his hands together with a soft clap. 'Where is the whiskey?' With a finger and thumb, he pointed at his brother-in-law. 'Thomas, find us the bottle and we'll make a toast.' He puffed out his chest. 'To the generations that went before us!'

'Do not give him that bottle, Thomas.' My mother's voice was one low note. 'You are not paying for the funeral, Felim, so you can go out and get your own whiskey.'

A man besieged, my father flicked his head from

Thomas to his wife, changing his expression like taffeta in full light or in shade. Thomas searched his pockets, patting himself down until he found a set of rosary beads and bowed his head in silent prayer. My father spread his fingers apart and held onto his knees. 'Dervla,' he said, closing his eyes, 'don't start.'

'Go on, Felim, remind us how you have suffered.' She stared into space as she taunted her husband, already bored with the game. 'It must be wonderful,' she went on, deliberately putting her head in the lion's mouth, 'to look down on us from your great height. Do we look very small from up there?'

We were back to this. The same scene, running on endlessly. I imagined my mother delivering Uncle Vanya's line – 'A lovely day for hanging yourself' – and getting a nervous laugh from the audience. To their credit, they played it as if they had not heard the words before: the disbelief, the hurt feelings, the amazement at each other came across as genuinely fresh. London had taught me something – I didn't have to tolerate it. The level of outrage in my father's voice was no longer convincing.

'Have I no right to expect some manners under my own roof? Is there no one left to stand up for decent behaviour? The two of you, ganging up on me. That's what I have to look forward to, is it?'

'It isn't,' my mother said.

My father turned on her, red-faced and fuming.

'That is exactly what it is! You, setting her against me. You've spent your life doing it.'

'It isn't *your* roof.' She pushed herself forwards, balancing on bent elbows, as though about to spring out of her

158

seat. 'Maybe you should have married my widowed mother instead of me, and then it would be.'

He floundered, eyes stinging. 'Dervla,' he whispered, 'God forgive you.' Speaking with his head lowered, he said, 'Your mother devoted her life to caring for you.'

'Caring for me? By letting me marry you? Was that caring for me?'

'Picking a fight over her dead body.' This thought riled him so much he pivoted his head and shoulders in my mother's direction. 'She's not even in the ground! Could you not have waited until she couldn't hear us, at least?'

'Hush up,' Veronica said, 'you'll wake the baby.'

'He'd be delighted to wake the baby, Vee.' My mother extended an arm towards her sister. 'Another witness to his martyrdom. Bring in the village and the county board, set him up on national television to broadcast his misfortune,' she crossed her hands over her heart, 'married to such a bitch.'

The thought that they never tired of telescoping old arguments together and making us listen to them suddenly upset me. To live in the same house, sleep in the same bed, with someone you couldn't stop punishing? The telescope spun around in my head. Is that what I did to myself?

'Can you hear yourselves?' I said. 'Are you ever going to let up?' Nobody responded. They went on talking over me and I was stuck there, like the pea in a whistle.

'There is no pleasing you, Dervla.' He sounded worn out. 'If I brought home a cake, you'd want me to eat it for you as well. You are not half the woman your mother was.'

I glanced over at Kathleen Mallon, lying serenely in her coffin, far, far away. My mother was shouting.

'You overgrown bullock. You bankrupt, scrounging, selfish waster. You think romance is a tactic: "I bought you something. Stop complaining." You signed for a house that I pay the mortgage on, if that's what you mean. Because paying debts and saving money is so boring. You couldn't begin to know what I want, Felim. It is beyond you.'

I half-expected a sound effect: a roll of thunder, a gunshot. A train hitting my body and finally uniting them in black crêpe and velvet, but this wasn't Russia in the 1890s. It was my parents in a cramped bungalow, in the same, depressing pattern they had worn for years. Badly stitched, puckered with too much tension, unaltered. Veronica had picked up a sod of turf with the fire tongs and held it, suspended, staring at her sister. She saw me watching her and turned her attention to stoking the grate.

'Is this,' I drew an infinity loop between my parents with a finger, 'what you want? To be married alive?'

'It takes four years to get divorced,' my mother said, too quickly. 'Where do you suggest we can live apart, for four years?'

That was new. My father sat back and deflated. 'We made a vow, Dervla.'

'It's 2002, not 1975,' my mother said. 'What am I talking about? You still believe in Adam and Eve. Everything that goes wrong in your life is my fault. Because I won't be your quiet little woman.' She threw up her hands and surveyed the ceiling. Unexpectedly, she pointed at me. 'If you get married, Mairéad, don't get sick or tired. He won't notice and he certainly won't take care of you. You got away because I made sure you did.'

Her pointing finger jabbed at my father. 'And he will make sure you never come home, won't you, Felim?'

Veronica took off her square-heeled suede shoe and flung it at the wall. 'Stop bickering. The pair of you. I don't want to hear it. No one wants to hear it.' She closed her eyes and may have tried to count to ten but couldn't hold it. 'Felim, maybe you should go.'

'No!' Thomas was on his feet, fists at his sides, lips pressed tightly together. He sank to his knees and took out his wooden beads. 'Let us pray,' he pleaded. 'The First Sorrowful Mystery—'

My mother shook her head at him. 'No, Tom. No more rosaries. We are past praying.'

When he began reciting the Hail Mary, she left her seat, knelt in front of her brother and gently stopped his hands. They were still for a moment, holding each other's reflection, before she spoke again.

'There is no heaven or hell. Mammy is dead. She is not watching over us. Mairéad is right, there is nothing more she can say.' Turning to my father, she leaned back a little to appraise him. There was a long silence, until she said, 'I think I married you because you charmed Mammy and it softened her hatred of me.'

This might be it, I thought. Felim and Dervla, making peace. He, shaking his head; she, nodding hers. The rest of us. Oh, for fuck's sake. Look at the rest of us, held in their orbit. They wanted to monopolise the attention of the whole room. I pictured myself walking out and not coming back.

'She did not hate you, Dervla.' Veronica sat, diddle-diddle-dumpling, one shoe off, one shoe on, crying for her sister or her mother, or both.

'Didn't she?' My mother picked up Veronica's missile and handed it back to her.

We heard the back door open and two voices, laughing together. Someone tried and failed to pull down the handle of the door to the kitchen that I had shut, once, twice, bursting through on the third attempt. Hugh, flushed and grinning, came to stand in front of Veronica.

'Does anyone mind?' He held a plate in one hand and pointed at it with a fork in the other. 'Does anyone mind if I have a go at this cheesecake? There's three of them out there. Three! Dan doesn't want it. He found a casserole! Nobody wants the cheesecakes. So, does anyone mind? Vee?'

He shared his grin with the rest of us, evidently pleased with his performance of a sober man, as Veronica put her shoe back on. She looked up at him and her whole body relaxed.

'Come out to the kitchen with me, you big eejit. Hand me the cake before you plant your face in it.'

My mother picked up her cigarettes and lighter and went out the opposite door as my father sat and watched her. Thomas wanted someone to sing 'The winter it is past', asking my father to begin. You imagine a wake as a moving farewell with the playing of uilleann pipes, a curlew calling from the water, sharing ballads and memories of the dead at their best. The reality is the same old songs being murdered as you sit with your anger and fatigue and wonder how you ended up like this, trading accusations, incapable of having a meaningful conversation. There was a black mark on the wall where Veronica had aimed the sharp heel. I hoped it would stay there.

Easter Monday, 1 April 2002

A nightmare woke me in the early hours: a gigantic wave bearing down on where I stood at the bottom of a steep gorge. The sight of the wave, rolling forward without breaking, would not leave me. I saw the height and force of the water each time I closed my eyes.

Felim and Thomas were sitting up with the coffin. Don't mention last night, I told myself. Fight and forget about it. How else could we live together? Share a packet of custard creams if we really wanted to put it behind us. My father watched me attempting to lie sideways on the couch, legs bent, knees hanging over the edge of the seat as my head drifted downwards, coming to land on the armrest. It wasn't as comfortable as it used to be, like getting on a child's swing and finding it pinched your hips.

'Do you remember Granny Kate's old horse, Dad?' I said to the upholstery. 'Rosie? Ruby?'

'Ruby,' he said.

'You used to say she drew sparks from the stones off the road.'

'Could have left you for a fortnight, standing at the fence, watching her. Did you want one?' he asked.

I lifted my head in surprise.

'A horse? Don't be daft. What would I have done with a horse?'

'I'm part-owner of a lovely mare. Klondike Bay. A syndicate.' He crossed his fingers over his stomach, looking immensely satisfied.

A racehorse. Naturally. Which meant he could go to every meeting on this island and the next.

'You've moved on from the dogs, Felim?' Thomas asked.

'Moving up in the world, Thomas. Progress. It's the only way.' He winked.

I let out a sharp laugh. Was there anything progressive about a single one of us? My father was not advancing. I could have asked him: How much have you spent on her? How much have you won? He might as well have planted the money in vegetable drills and expected a crop from it. If Mum left him, he would end up living in his van.

'Is the Grand National on today?' I asked and saw his fingers twitch, his lips pursed. He passed his hand over his cheeks, rasping the stubble. Had he made his bet yesterday? Did he need to make another one? A horse race or a funeral? Which one did he love more?

'Aye, it is.' He examined the carpet for a moment, probably trying not to think about what he was missing. When he lifted his face towards me, I could see he had already bounced back. Who wouldn't warm to him?

'How is Liz Taylor, in London? Was she asking for me?'

'Pining,' I said. 'Her and Julie Christie. They'll never get over you.'

'You could bring someone home with you sometime. Get yourself a nice fella.'

He meant, Get someone white and preferably Irish.

'That was a bad bit of PR for *nice fellas* like you last night,' I replied, feeling my jaw tightening. 'Could put people off married life altogether.'

'Have you visited your cousins in Surbiton lately?'

'Dad. I went along with your idea. I visited them, and they were very generous with their oppression. I'm not going back. "You should get involved with your local parish. Do you know where we met? At Mass! What do you mean, you don't go?" They were relentless. "Do you smoke cannabis? Have you taken cocaine? Do you know about the young Irish woman who came over here, took cocaine from a stranger and ended up on her own with a black baby? Why don't you join a Gaelic football team? Plenty of women play nowadays. Wouldn't it keep you off the streets?" Sweet suffering Jesus, I couldn't get out of there fast enough.'

He, the cousin, had dismissed whatever I said, pushing my answers further and further away, to the point of being lost. They wanted to bury me in nappies and housework and then tell me how happy I should be.

'Stop that, Mairéad. They are your family.'

'No, they're *your* family. What would you do if I brought home a black baby, Dad? Would you show us off down at the pub?'

'Remember the Reliant?' Thomas almost shouted.

We both looked at him. I had interrupted their time alone. If Granny were here, I would have been sent to do something in the kitchen. My father took a second to readjust, to ignore my question.

'I do, Thomas. But I wanted a Capri,' he replied.

They were talking about cars they had owned. My mother said they would spend more time poring over a vintage-car calendar than one of naked women. Because they loved cars. I closed my eyes and returned to half-lying on the couch. What my father had said last night – 'It doesn't suit you, being smart with me' – it didn't suit him, that was what he disliked. I had made a scene and I was beginning to understand why my mother did it; to expose the possibility that he might be wrong. It was his choice to get thick. His choice, not my fault. Let them exclude me. It was almost morning.

The undertakers arrived in dark suits and quiet shoes. Veronica gave the nod to fix the lid onto the coffin while we recited 'Hail, Holy Queen, Mother of Mercy, hail, our life our sweetness and our hope'. I felt the screws twisting in my throat. It was a joke, a terrible prank, a slap in the mouth. Vee had asked me at breakfast: How many cakes of soda bread did Mammy make in this kitchen? How many pounds of butter? My appetite shrank as I sat at the table, staring at the teapot, apologising for wearing the same outfit as the day before.

She offered me her spare coat for the funeral Mass. Anything to cover up what I had on was welcome. Even a brass-buttoned, full-length military monster. The flap pockets were fake and there was nowhere to hide my hands as we prayed. I hugged my ribs, pressing hard against the heavy material as they manoeuvred my grandmother from the sitting-room to the hall, out the front door and into the open hearse. I had not expected to be so overwhelmed, watching her leave. As they secured the coffin for the drive to the church, a hand on my shoulder was my father instructing me to walk tall, the same way Granny Kate did.

Veronica's family went in the first car, then the rest of us. Mum driving, Thomas beside her, me and Dad in the back. I concentrated on memorising the journey, framed by the car window, as if I were doing it for Kathleen Mallon.

A small crowd watched us getting out at the church, bells tolling, the undertaker organising the pallbearers. Why had I bought such ugly shoes? My dad, dignified in his good coat, and Hugh were the anchormen as they carried the coffin down the centre aisle to its stand in front of the altar. Mum and I walked behind the rest of the family and took the second pew, where she gestured for me to keep moving further along, to free up some space, and I ended up too close to an old radiator as hot as a coal fire. The priest was only on the preliminaries and already I felt dizzy and afraid to stand. Reluctantly, I took off the monster coat, exposing the awful purple jumper underneath. The shame of it seemed to increase my temperature and I felt nauseous. When I stayed seated for the Gospel, my mum leaned down and asked me what was wrong.

'Take off your jumper,' she whispered, but I shook my head. Impossible. Back fat on view. Sweat stains. I'd rather collapse and be carried out.

'Mum,' I said, pinching her sleeve, 'I can't do the prayer.'

I had to put my head between my knees at the thought of standing at the altar and speaking. Perhaps because my face was green or my voice so faint, she didn't chide me.

She stood up, tapped Veronica's shoulder in the row in front, said something quickly in her ear and turned back to me.

'Can you walk?'

Picking up the massive coat, she put her arm around my waist and we moved as swiftly as we could manage down the outside aisle. There was an exit in the transept to my right and my mother steered me through the arched doorway and into the fresh air. I spat the bile gathered in my mouth into a gutter drain. There were no benches but there was a low wall nearby with a cherry tree coming into bloom overhead. She sat me underneath it and then sat down herself. I took off the stupid jumper and immediately felt better. From her handbag, she took a fistful of mint humbugs and told me to take them. I didn't want to, but took one to please her.

'Thanks, Mum. You can go back in, if you want. I'm fine here.'

'No, thanks. I'm fine here too.' She unwrapped a humbug, put it in her mouth, and waited for me to do the same. 'Dan will do your prayer.'

In his broad Mayo vowels. Good. I tried to hold the boiled sweet in the middle of my tongue and taste as little as possible. Glucose. Palm oil. Emulsifier. 'I'll never live it down, leaving Granny's funeral Mass. That's all they'll say about me today.'

'Another black mark for us, isn't it? We'll surely burn for this one.' She twisted the cellophane wrapper into a tight rope between her fingers. 'Promise me you won't have this charade when I die. Have a wake if you want to, but don't take me to a church.'

There was a gentle scent of pink blossoms from the tree and I took slow, deep breaths of it.

'Do you want to be buried?' I asked.

'Well, I'll be dead, so it won't matter. Just don't involve the clergy, if you can help it.'

'Because?'

'Because I can't stand the bigots and hypocrites.' The venom in her tone made my temperature drop. 'Go in there,' she continued, the sweet knocking against her teeth, 'and ask them what happens to homosexuals or to women who use contraception or to fornicators, which just means prostitutes, when they die. Are they granted eternal rest, O Lord?'

I put the jumper back on and the monster coat under my bum. She wasn't finished.

'Do you want to hear a joke?' she asked, turning to face me without smiling. 'Christian Ireland.'

I thought she had paused, but then she laughed at her statement.

'Is that the joke? I don't get it,' I said.

'Make sure you have money before you come home, Mairéad. They will love you if you have money. See how the rich are worshipped in this country, forgiven all their sins. But there are some things you cannot buy. The best experiences can come to you when you haven't a penny to your name. The stuffed shirts around here will never get it. They will tell you it's not the shoes they gave you that are too small, it's your feet that are too big.'

I felt cold and lonely listening to her, unwilling to follow the rant. There was no room for me here. Was she angry at her mother for being dead, or had death just made her furious in general? How would she get through the hotel reception after the burial without another slagging match with my father? The syrup gathering around my bottom teeth was bringing on another bout of nausea. I spat the half-sucked sweet back into its wrapper and ran my tongue over my new fillings to get rid of the sugar.

'What's wrong with it?' She frowned at me.

'Nothing. I've just had enough.' I closed my fist around the sticky mess and asked: 'Mum, did you eat anything for breakfast?'

'I had tea.'

Tea and sweets and cigarettes. Probably little else for the past few days. No wonder she was short-tempered.

'You didn't cut up a grapefruit for me today.'

It was my fault she had consumed no solids.

'I didn't cut that grapefruit yesterday. Dad did.'

'He did not. Did he? Well. I see.' She pressed her lips together and puffed through her nostrils. The sweet knocked against her teeth again and she stared into the middle distance.

'Granny Kate used to give me a boiled egg with brown bread and marmalade in the mornings. Sometimes it was honey, if she ran out of marmalade. And margarine. Big, square tubs of that slop on the kitchen table. That was some cod, wasn't it? Margarine.' Did she stifle a yawn? Was I boring her? 'What was Granny like when you were growing up?'

'Mammy was different with all of us. Veronica and Thomas, they didn't see the sides of her that I did.' Her face was still turned away from me.

'But why do you think she hated you? What you said last night, that Dad blames you for whatever misfortune happens to him, isn't that what you do with Granny?' It would help her to hear this, I thought, taking a moment to congratulate myself. My mother sighed and closed her eyes.

'Marmalade and honey? No, darling, not for me. Did you hear what she did when Felim asked me to marry him and I said no? She stopped eating. Refused to touch a bite until I changed my mind. Saying decades of the rosary for me every time I looked at her. Or so I thought. She told Felim afterwards that she had dry toast when I wasn't there. Then, when you were born, she said to me: "Make them feel guilty. Tell them to go ahead and do what they want, no matter who it upsets. That's how you get children to behave."'

With the heel of her palm on her forehead, she spoke to the patch of ground between her feet: 'I couldn't tell her anything. She didn't want to hear it. It's hard enough to have a conversation with a saint when they're alive. There will be no one who will want to listen to me now she's dead.'

It was true that a lot of subjects had been taboo for my grandmother. Especially if it related to the body, to nakedness or to sex. The denials could make my mother outrageous. There was one summer's day, haymaking weather, when my great-aunt sat outside with her sister, my grandmother, while I pretended to serve them tea in imaginary cups. Mum was on a fold-out sun lounger, resting. I must have been running around in the heat, because my mother said I could take off my top to let the air at my skin. Whatever was said next was enough to make her sit up and point a finger at both of the older women, stating that she would not let them do

171

this again. She stood and, this is why I remember it, pulled off her sundress and threw it down in front of her mother. When she began to take off her underwear, the sisters got up together and went inside in silence. There is nothing shameful about your body, she told me, but that wasn't what she believed of herself. Too many layers had been turned into stone. Their opposition had remained fixed in place, daughter against mother. Possibly the only way they could relate was for one to make the rules, the other to defy them. The sudden outbursts were followed by a return to order. My mother was not a revolutionary.

The service was coming to an end. Smokers were walking straight out after Communion and going around the far side of the church. Iggy was one of them. I stood up and put the coat back on as soon as I saw him. He either didn't see me or didn't want to see me. 'Jesus, Remember Me' drifted our way. One of the undertakers appeared and opened the boot of the hearse, parked in front of the north-facing doors. The coldest place to have the main entrance, where everyone would congregate to shake hands and sympathise, and I could stand in the wind and comfortably button myself in. We walked towards the procession of men – the priest, the altar boys, the pallbearers – breathing in frankincense.

'Here they come to tell me what a wonderful woman she was.' She lowered her voice as we approached the hearse. 'What do they know? She wasn't their mother.'

Veronica came directly to me and asked what happened, why did we leave? I told her it was a false alarm, I thought I was going to vomit. She kissed my cheek and held me tightly and I wanted to bury my face and let the tears come, but a woman pressed her hand on Veronica's shoulder, turning her around.

'She was a lady, was Kate. A great loss. I had sepsis twenty years ago and didn't know it, but she got me to the hospital quick-smart. The tip of a thorn, they said, could have killed me. I don't suppose she told you, did she? No. Too modest. Well. I'm sorry for your trouble, Veronica. I'll say a prayer for you.'

A clamour of people came forward to share their sorrow, to mention an incident, to say nothing but grip my hand and squeeze my elbow. They recognised me, saying: 'You're Dervla's, aren't you?' It felt like death was right here, lacing its needle and thread through the air. Had they thought about their own funeral, as I had, when they saw my grandmother's coffin? When my turn to wake alone in the dark came, would it find me scared of dying, heartbroken that everything would go on without me? A school friend approached, reminding me how her mother knew mine. She attempted to bring us both up to date on who was doing what now, but I was scanning the scene behind her, searching for Iggy over the heads of the sympathisers. I couldn't see him.

The graveyard was a short walk from the church. In the cortège behind the hearse, I fell into step with my mother and we stood together at the freshly dug plot, smelling of damp earth, awaiting the Rite of Committal. A blessing of the grave, a short service bidding the dead to sleep until the Resurrection, a grateful whisper that the rain had held off. I had never experienced any type of funeral but this. The only ending I knew was to pray in unison as we put the body in the ground. When the pallbearers began lowering the coffin by woven straps into the six-foot hole, I pulled my mother close with an arm around her waist. I heard Thomas cry to Veronica, 'What will we do without her?' Veronica made no reply.

I wanted to tell my grandmother something, wishing I had known her mother and grandmother who each had a daughter. Had they once desired a feathered trilby, gold embroidery, silk next to their skin instead of worn-out cotton? Did they long to wear linen in summer, fine wool in winter and steadily unpick the stiff borders they had been stitched into? Were they frightened of what they wanted? My mother gripped my hand, watching them cover the wooden lid with a scattering of clay. We are no different, I thought. We are all afraid of something.

My cousin Brian was standing with Iggy in the hotel foyer. I froze for a second at the sight of Iggy, thrilled he had come, worried it was not for me. Brian was doing the talking, without a trace of an American accent, despite his nine years of living there.

'Granny always got the turkey and ham from Keogh's. Couldn't top them, she said. She was very sorry when your dad passed away.'

The suit with the black tie. It must have been what Iggy wore to his father's funeral. That I was not here for. I remembered the sound of his belt buckle, a metallic *ting-ting-ting*ing, when he lifted his jeans off the floor. He used to kiss my crown to say goodbye and I wanted him to repeat the gesture, to bring back that sensation. I went up to them.

'I didn't see you at the church, Iggy. I mean, I did, but.' I didn't know what I meant.

'It was some crowd,' he said, looking at Brian. 'Your grandmother would have been pleased.'

Hugh was at the entrance to the Function Room, pausing with his hands on his hips. 'Brian! Over here, son, there's someone I want you to meet.'

Brian gave his dad a thumbs-up. 'That fella never stops. It'll either be an old footballer or someone who wants to talk about cattle. Why don't you come in? There's plenty of food. Don't be shy.' He put one hand on my arm, the other on Iggy's, and made to steer us through the double doors, but I took a tiny step backwards, wriggling lightly out of his grip.

'Quick cigarette and I'll be with you,' Iggy said, patting the contents of his inside pocket. Brian looked disappointed in Iggy, but he left us alone.

'Come outside with me?' he asked, when Brian was out of sight.

'You're going outside to smoke?' I said, then realised I was being thick.

The Portrush cousins were coming in, my father with them. They'd go to the bar, then the Function Room, and no one would be spared their company. There was a green emergency exit sign on the wall.

'Let's go out the fire doors over there.' Not wanting to turn around and get trapped by the relatives behind me, I walked off without waiting for Iggy to agree.

We leaned on a windowsill on the sunny side of the building. I had once again removed myself from the family group. You could say it was becoming a pattern.

'Do you go to the funerals of many customers? Is it good for business?'

He was taken aback. 'Why would you say that? I knew your grandmother and I liked her. She was a lady.'

'Unlike me?'

There was some fussing with his tie, lifting it up, smoothing it flat. This was not going as he had planned. He opened, then closed his mouth. And opened it again.

'You left for London without telling me.'

My mind was blank. I remembered getting on a bus, my rucksack in the hold, and falling asleep like a child in the back seat. Had I thought about Iggy? Possibly not.

'Did I? Why did you want me to? Were you planning to come with me?' It was a joke. But suddenly it wasn't. I was shocked at how much I wanted it, after I said it, to have someone who cared about what happens to me, who would hold my hand and kiss my head. The endless benefits for me. What would it do to him?

'Is it lonely?' he asked, with unexpected kindness. I had to stare over the tops of the hydrangea bushes in front of us and focus on the parked cars beyond them. If it had started raining, it would have been a relief.

I thought about when I had interrupted Lou Hao in his dressingroom while he was admiring his naked chest in the mirror before a show: 'If you can't appreciate your own body, sweetheart, how are you going to let someone else do it?' I hadn't let Iggy rest his hands on me, not really. I didn't want him to touch my fat places; it had felt horrible, like being backed into a corner by wasps. I regretted that.

'Yes.'

'Do you want to come home?'

'Eventually.' In some distant, perfect future. What would

I do here, except fail? 'Do you remember sitting by the river, mitching off school?'

'Aye,' he said, smiling. 'Doing our biology homework.'

'The last time,' I said. Not my finest hour: foul-mouthed, angry at him for something he did or didn't say. 'Iggy, you never asked me out, you know? We just hooked up when we were drunk. Your friends definitely didn't like me and I thought you were killing time with me, until something better came along.'

He shifted away on the sill, crossing one leg over the other. 'I think you know I wasn't.'

No, I did not. I wasn't sure what he felt; I wasn't sure what I felt.

'You're engaged,' I said.

'You should come home, if you want to come home,' he said.

Did he miss me? I almost sank to the ground, head in hands, at the thought of the loneliness I was going back to, at the impossibility of staying here, where the options were getting married or getting married. Instead, I pressed down on my palms to push myself upright, turning to face his square shoulders, his blue, blue eyes.

'I should go inside,' I said. 'I already skipped the Mass, I'd better not avoid this part as well.'

'If that's what you want.' He returned my stare for a long moment and did not move.

Veronica wanted to get some fresh air and put on her walking shoes when we returned to the house. Thomas said he was going up to the barn, which is where he went to smoke. My mother went inside and locked herself in the bathroom, screaming uncontrollably as soon as the door was closed. The noise went on and on, as if she didn't know how to stop. I sat outside, waiting, not sure if I was doing the right thing. Amy came to watch me. She would have no memories of her great-grandmother, only what we told her. She'd be an image in a photograph to her. Amy heard the screaming, but she didn't say a word. I could see the delicate child-hairs on her plump arms and her cheeks as she came in close to examine the bruise around my eye, then she wandered off again.

The lock was released on the bathroom door and my mother stood for a moment, one hand pushing the frame. She looked shattered. Her eyes were red and swollen and her face was dreadfully pale. Whatever she felt or thought when she saw me sitting on the floor, she was not able to say. She ran her hand along the wall, moving slowly until she reached a bedroom, went in and lay down to rest.

Tuesday morning, 2 April 2002

My mother drove me back to Knock Airport. Sheep grazed along the verges of the exposed road leading to the terminal building. The blobs of red dye on their fleece were too vivid against the bracken and heather. Anything attempting to grow upwards was blown sideways by the wind.

'I won't go in,' she said, after she had parked. 'Are you all right for money?'

Veronica had pressed some folded notes into my hand as she said goodbye. My first time to handle euro.

'Veronica gave me a few quid towards the flight.' The notes were smaller than what I was used to. 'I did bring my own cash, but it's old money. There was no time to exchange it.' I tried to estimate how much was in the pencil case I'd grabbed when I was leaving London. 'Will you take it, before it's useless?'

She took out her purse from her handbag and tipped the contents of my pencil case into it, giving me a fifty-euro note in return.

'Take it,' she ordered, and then gripped the steering wheel with both hands.

The silences were back. I was thinking about my home

economics teacher, Mrs Corrigan, and her red Toyota, who showed me how to cut a pattern, how to thread a sewing-machine. When I tried to make a dress, I stitched the sleeves on back to front and the darts at the bust were at different levels. 'Frog it,' Ms Corrigan said. 'Rip it out and start over. You'll be quicker the second time round.'

'Do you remember the set of cushion covers I made for you, Mum, when I was in first year at secondary school?'

'I do. You did a lovely job on the seams, so lovely you left no opening to put the cushions into them.'

'And you didn't mention it. I only realised what I'd done when I saw the zips you added.' How does anyone manage to say what they mean? 'You left a voicemail on my phone last week. Wondering if I had vanished altogether.'

'It's what I would do, if I were your age. You don't have to be the fastest, just faster than the dog that's chasing you.'

'Sometimes, often, I don't know what to say to people, so I run away. It's not— You can't outrun a dog, Mum, that's not possible.' I was confusing myself, struggling from lack of sleep, but I couldn't go back to London without trying to tell my mother how I felt, to stop myself from worrying that she would die next and I had missed my chance. 'I feel trapped when I'm here, or not the right shape. I don't fit. And I don't fit in London either. I have the wrong hair, the wrong teeth, I cannot stand up to them: nothing I do is enough. Dad told me to bring someone home with me, for his approval. Which would he like best, if I fell in love and wanted to live happily ever after with a British army officer, a Muslim, or a woman? What do you think?'

'Falling in love is not happiness,' my mother said.

I waited. Was that her conclusion? I was becoming fed up with evasions, fed up with her covering her copybook with a forearm in case anyone would dare to read her mind.

'Did you get married because you were pregnant?' I said, unable to keep the anger in.

'Shut up, Mairéad.' The sharpness in her voice didn't surprise me. She would either start shouting or clam up. Throwing her arms into the air, she barked, 'It had nothing to do with you. You didn't exist. There was a time, believe it or not, when I was not your mother.' She lifted her face to the sky, swallowing the next line.

'How am I supposed to know what you haven't told me? Whatever it was, you might as well say it, because I won't be home again for a long while.' I heard my voice rising and thought maybe I was overreacting. We kept secrets from each other, so what? She had not demanded to hear mine. There were plenty of rewards for lying; keep head-butting people for answers and you would get yourself excluded. Permanently. Except, I couldn't stop. I wanted to kill this secret that was making us sick, the one that had kept her waiting up for me on summer nights, smoking in the dark at the kitchen table, furious with me for whatever I had, or had not, done. The way my parents looked at each other with hatred. The tension in their house that would burst an appendix. I pushed on.

'Was there another woman?' The question came from exasperation. Something I had wondered about my father in the past, but had never asked. It provoked her more than I intended. Her face reddened, a tear spilled out, then another, until she closed her eyelids to contain the rest. When she opened them again, she pointed her finger at me.

'You will tell no one. Not a sinner.'

'Mum,' I said, 'is that all it was?'

Her watch had a slim, mother-of-pearl clock face and a thin metal strap, the better to show off the smallness of her wrist. She was opening and closing the tiny clasp. Opening and closing. Her finger and thumb performed the trick automatically, with no assistance, something I had not known any actor to be able to do.

'"Is that all?" this child asks me. Is that all? Easy knowing you didn't live through it. Marriage was compulsory in my day. Daughters did not inherit. You cannot understand what it was like.'

'I can't understand because you won't let me,' I said.

A bit more staring out the side window, a bit more fiddling with her watch.

'I worked with her in a guesthouse on the Shannon. Earning our boat fare to emigrate, or so we thought. We slept in those poky attic rooms, too small to stand up in. Rising at cock-crow. My first job was to get the range lit and she'd start on the breakfasts. I still cook eggs the way she showed me. She gave me her good coat.'

Her fist went into her mouth and she appeared to be biting down hard on her fingers. It was distressing to watch and I was going to tell her to stop. If she wanted to, she could stop. Her breathing became rapid and shallow. I watched her bring it under control, moving the air from the top of her lungs to the bottom. Patches of fog grew larger on the windscreen.

'We did not talk about sex back then. There was no education, apart from what you saw the animals doing on the farm but, I . . . I was very innocent. Another woman might tell you to "Watch out for him" or take your arm and escort you away, but we had no words to put on it. I thought I could keep out of trouble. I was smart, I could avoid him. Dodging around tables and keeping my back to the wall.' She stared at her lap and said in a voice that was high and quiet: 'I was so young.' When she lifted her head again, I could see her jaw harden. 'They put down a bull if it starts to attack. I wish I'd poisoned the fucker with arsenic.'

Something was oozing in my stomach and at the back of my mouth. 'Who?' I asked.

'I was standing at the big kitchen sink, up to my elbows in dishwater.' She was using that sharp tone, the *stop whingeing and get up* tone. 'I heard him come in, the great Mr Walsh, singing "Whiskey on a Sunday". The next thing, I felt his hand up my skirt. I didn't understand what he was doing, or what I was supposed to do. I wasn't. I didn't—' She halted, exhaled and continued. 'I wasn't wearing any knickers.'

This was not what I wanted. I had no desire to listen to a horror story, not from my mother. I leaned forward to pick up my bag and started saying, 'Mum, you don't have to.'

Abruptly, she raised her voice. 'Have you any idea how hot a kitchen is in summer? With your face over boiling water, under a grill, over a pan? We sweated through every article of clothing; my feet would be like tree stumps. I couldn't bear to wear tights; they gave me thrush.' She dragged her nails along the hairline above her ears and then pushed the fingertips into her scalp. 'You said you wanted to know.'

'I did. But, Mum—'

'No one else has ever wanted to know.'

The layer of breath-fog had spread from the windscreen to cover the middle of all the car windows. Around the edges where the glass was clear, I could see the airport control tower and an orange windsock. She would have a long drive back on her own. 'Go on,' I said.

'He put his hand around my throat and all of his weight was at my back. Then I felt his mouth open, his lips were touching my neck and his fingers were pushing. Into.'

The first boy to put his fingers inside me was six years older and I would have died rather than tell my mother. The idea of it made me reach for the door handle. She pressed my thigh firmly. What I understood was that she was not trying to warn me. No one warned us in time; we did not know this could happen until it happened to us. She had to say it out loud to break its power over her thoughts. Let the terror become anger.

'You think I should have screamed or elbowed him in the balls or stabbed him with a fork? Well, I did none of those things. It went on and on until she came in and slammed down a tray of dishes, saying, "Everything all right, sorr?" *Sorr*, she said, and it was as sour as his breath. The dirty bastard unhooked himself. "Tiptop," he said.' She looked at her watch as if she could see it happening again. 'Tiptop. The prick. I could *hear* him smiling. I should have screamed. I should have run into the dining-room and told everyone Mr Walsh had put his hand up my skirt and he a married man.'

Before I could move again, she tightened her grip on my thigh.

'When it happens to you, you can tell me what you did and what I should have done. Because what I did, at that moment, was to put my head down and get on with the washing-up.'

She released the pressure on my leg. We both began to cry.

'How did you get away?'

'He woke me up in the middle of the night, clamping a hand over my mouth. "Stay still and I won't hurt you. It'll be worse if you move," he said. It was so dark, I couldn't see properly. His hand was as big as a shovel. The smell, Jesus Christ. He stank. Rotten teeth, rotten everything. I tried to grab the sides of the bed, but my fingers got caught between the springs and the frame. The bruises came up as hard little knots of black and blue. Snot was coming out my nose and I thought I was suffocating and he went on grunting.' She started pinching her knuckles and kneading the flesh below them. 'That nonsense about virginity. Checking if a woman is *intact* before she gets married? All lies. Any man who thinks we are sealed like a parcel is an ignorant gobshite. How could you bleed every month, if you were closed over? There was no blood soaking the sheets. Only semen. And inside. Inside, I was sore. Red, raw, sore.'

I waited, watching her pick up and open a packet of tissues from the door pocket on the driver's side. The funeral director's name was stickered across the plastic. Part of the burial service. I remembered her thumb stroking the back of my hand as a child, weaving tiny patterns to soothe me. My mother. Red nail polish. Lipstick. Rage. Falling backwards down a well and there was nothing to hold, no one to haul her out, only the sound of wind in a tunnel.'She had heard something. Found me in the kitchen, hiding. Perished. "Go," she told me. "Go now, before the devil wakes up." She gave me her beautiful gabardine and set me walking out the door and into the dawn. Without my wages. Without anything except what I was standing up in. People think it's a joke, a woman falling in love with another woman. "How could you manage without a little pink willy?" Well, I can understand it. She helped me more than anyone else in my whole life. She was saving up. Going to emigrate to New Zealand. As far as you could get from—' A wave of her hand, banishing something. 'I walked for hours to get home. Mammy wanted to send me straight back. I didn't tell her what happened. I cycled into town every day and read the advertisements until I saw the job in the café, got on the next bus to Sligo and landed on the doorstep. Could I take the orders and manage the till? Of course I could. "Aren't you a great girl?" Mrs Madigan said, and took me on. When they closed down, I started at the super-market.'

'What happened to him? Mr Walsh?'

She snorted. 'I went back and chopped off his fingers one by one. I cut out his tongue. I put his picture in the paper along with the names of every girl he had harmed. What do you think? Nothing happened to him.' A slap of her palm on the steering wheel set my heart racing. 'I told you to shut up. Why can you not do as you're told?' This made her laugh. 'Why? Because you're smarter than me. That's why. And I'm glad of it.'

I did not turn away. The sense that she always wanted more and more from me, and never stopped expecting me to do what she could not, had pushed me as far as London. Without thinking of what it had cost her. I had also thought I was smart, that I could avoid becoming like her.

'That's not true, Mum. I got to stay at school for longer, is all.' My ridiculous bag was sitting on my ridiculous shoes and I felt like a clown in my purple polo neck. 'I'm going back to London to wash clothes for a living and sleep in a house that has biographies of Margaret Thatcher in the front room. Signed by Margaret Thatcher and the author.' She did not find this as funny as I did. 'You'd like the theatre. They take in runaways and no one ever asks why I don't go to Mass.'

'It would have been better if I'd told you about the—If I'd told you at the right time.'

'Is this not the right time?'

She gave me a bright smile and said, 'I'm going to divorce your father. Sooner or later. Probably sooner.'

'Do it while you're still young,' I replied.

Her face softened. I made to leave the car once more, then hesitated.

'What was her name, the woman who helped you?'

'Mairéad,' she said.

I picked up her hand and held it tight. 'I'm sorry,' I said, and I meant it. 'I'm sorry.'

She put her other hand over mine and whispered, 'I know.'

London

Tuesday, 2 April 2002

On the return flight, fat, salt tears poured down my cheeks for as long as we were airborne. A steward brought me tea and rubbed my arm without speaking. The man next to me had a delicate stutter and left a section of his ham sandwich beside the tea, patiently encouraging me to eat some or to take a drink. I told him I was coming back from a funeral. 'I'll say a prayer for you,' he said.

On the Tube back to Kingsbury, a tall man sat opposite, wide-legged, and turned down the corners of his mouth as he looked at me. I had slumped down in my tired, homesick body with my legs out, feet flexed. I wanted to use my strong, articulate foot to lift him by the crotch and fling him out of the door, to use my knee to channel the power of my thigh into his lower abdomen until he had difficulty sitting up, spreading his legs and judging women.

When I got back to the house, it was empty, and it felt like I was the one who had stayed behind while everyone else moved away. My boss, Margaret – English, intimidating Margaret – who had never been to Ireland, had sent a sympathy card. It was waiting for me on the kitchen table. An image of the Madonna and child in golden yellow and ultramarine, and she wrote: *Forgive my insensitivity, for blurting it out on the phone. I am sorry I did that. I am so sorry your grandmother has died.* I swayed a little, held the back of a chair, and felt something being slowly, painfully taken from me.

A small figure knocked on the square of yellow glass in the back door and then stood where I could see her in the garden. Mrs Hanif. Fatima. Holding a lunch box and a package in tin foil. I invited her in to the kitchen.

'Hannah told Samira about your fall. And your nani dying. This dhal is for you. Very nourishing.'

The sides of the lunch box were warm as I took it from her. 'Thank you.'

'And chapati. My own.' She pointed to the foil parcel on top.

I wanted to say more, to offer her something in return for her gift, for coming to check on me.

'I broke the cupboard door,' is what came hurtling out of my mouth.

She waved her arms to stop me. 'Just an old hinge. Shadaan has repaired it. See?'

The door was hanging straight, as if the accident had not happened, but it came rushing back to me: waking up on the ground, the crooked door, the blood on the back of my head. I squeezed the lunch box while slowly blinking the images away.

'You look pale, my dear.' Fatima cupped her hand around my cheek and hummed sympathetically as she tapped her fingertips under my bruised eye socket. 'It is a difficult time.'

When she had returned through the side entrance to

her house next door, it occurred to me that she had also left her home, her mother, her grandmother.

Philippa answered the phone when I called Wardrobe.

'I can make it in for tonight's show.'

'Oh bloody hell, yes, please do! I'll let Margaret know you're coming.'

The joy in her voice. I had never known her to be so animated. The two shows on Saturday and one yesterday. Had she covered the gaps herself? Racing behind the stage? I'd missed out on bank-holiday pay. Not the end of the world, as long as I hadn't been replaced altogether. I emptied my travelling bag onto my bed, changed into blue jeans and the Breton stripes and left for work.

There was plenty of time to get off the Tube at Bond Street and walk. I turned from Oxford Street onto Regent Street, looking boldly at the window displays. I was going to buy something decent to wear. Something that fitted me. About halfway down the hill, I saw a black dress on a mannequin. Three-quarter-length sleeves, boat-neck collar, darts at the bust. Darts at the bust! I went inside and found the rail where three copies hung. Silk crêpe. Button details on the side of the shoulder and waist. I took two of the three sizes to a fitting-room and put one arm into a sleeve. I could test it without getting undressed. Tight sleeves meant I wouldn't be able to close it across my chest or get it over my hips. If I could get my arm through, it was worth trying it on properly. This one was not too tight; in fact, the underarm area was loose. I went for the full effect. The zip at the back closed smoothly. It had deep, angled pockets. My arms went in up to the wrist. This dress.

The cloth that could cure me. The last thing I did was to check the price tag. £950. The gambler in me wanted it very badly, working out the cost divided by the number of times I would wear it and the person I would become in it. If I had worn it at the funeral. If I could step out in something like this every day. My shares in a racehorse. The promise of it was strong, but I absolutely could not afford to buy. An assistant approached me as I walked back across the shop floor.

'It's beautiful, isn't it?' She was wearing a knee-length wool dress. Immaculate hair and make-up. I wondered if she had to pay for that from her wages.

'Very,' I said, handing it over. This wasn't my dress, but I knew what I wanted. When I was next on Berwick Street, or shopping for good material, I'd find it. Enough to make one dress and several pairs of short shorts that I'd pair with black tights for work. I could feel how much cooler they would be to move in, how much easier than jeans.

I hoped the first person I met at the theatre would be Mr Henderson. Get through the doors and it would be easier from then on. The first person was Lloyd, up a ladder, replacing lights under the canopy.

'Hello, Irish.' His gold tooth flashed in the sunlight.

'Doing some work? Things have changed since I was away.'

'I heard about your grandma.' He climbed down to the bottom rung. 'You all right, sweetheart?'

'I am, thanks, Lloyd.'

'Can I ask about the shiner? Was it something or someone?'

'Walked into a cupboard door. Seriously. Before I knew about my granny dying.'

He gave a low whistle. 'Before your brain knew, maybe. It goes deep, that connection. My grandma was very good to me. I was thinking about her, you know, because of the Queen Mother.' Tipping a lamp towards me, he had a realisation. 'There's your grandma and Bonnie Prince Charlie's passing on the same day. Nobody gets out alive, do they?' His good humour faded slightly. 'Slipping me money, feeding me up. I still miss her and she's dead thirty years.' There was a pause as he allowed the thought to hang for a moment. 'She used to play the piano. Loved a party. Had a voice like Shirley Bassey. Ah, you think I'm exaggerating, but I mean it. She could have been something.'

'Funeral was yesterday and there wasn't half enough singing.'

'You bury them quickly in Ireland, don't you?'

'There wasn't much talk about the Queen Mother at home. That might be a slightly different funeral.'

'Lying-in-state, in Westminster Hall. That's what they do, but not until Friday. Dead for a week by then. There'll be hundreds there, believe you me. Dead for a week. And her daughter gone to the grave just before her. You've got to take your chances when they come.' He climbed off the ladder and stared up at the canopy with his hands on his hips.

'Are you all right, Lloyd?'

He spoke upwards to the new lamps. 'Found out my ex-wife is getting remarried, didn't I? And, do you know what? I'm happy for her.' There was a drop of his shoulders, a gentle smile, as he lowered his gaze to the ground. 'Yes, sweetheart, I am.'

195

'Lloyd . . . That is, I'm sorry.'

'No, my love, we don't have the time to be sorry. Got to get on with it, don't you?'

I didn't reply because I was watching Anya walking out through Stage Door, followed by a woman of a similar build. They linked arms and continued what seemed to be a confidential conversation. Anya spoke quietly, right up until she halted in front of me.

'Margaret told me your grandmother is dead.' Her tone was flat and a worried look crossed her face.

'She is,' I said.

Anya patted the forearm of the woman with her. 'This is Marie, my sister.' She turned to her sister and said something in their own language. Her sister's mouth made an 'O' as Anya spoke and then she stepped forward and hugged me tightly for a second before holding me at arm's length. She was smiling, but her eyes were sad.

'You're not from London,' I said.

Anya laughed. 'One week, every year, she visits from Romania. We do a little shopping, go to a show, talk about home.'

Marie put her hand over her heart. 'Marie,' she said, patting her chest. 'It is my grandmother's name.' She hugged me once more in a strong, swift movement, pressing my arms to my sides to release me, as though she had turned me right side up. I returned her sad smile.

'We missed you,' Mr Henderson said.

'Snap,' was the most I could manage in reply. Keeping my head down, I climbed the stairs and went straight to Margaret's office. The door was open.

She started talking without looking up from her work.

196

Perhaps she knew my footsteps. Or my smell. 'You did the right thing, going back to Ireland.' There was a gold chain in her hands and she was worrying at a tangle of knots in the centre. 'We give up too much for this place. Must the show go on? Really? Vomiting bugs. Broken bones. Miscarriages. Forcing people to perform when they are in pain. It is wrong. I didn't always believe that, but the older I get, the more I realise.'

I wasn't sure if I was meant to leave or to stay and listen. Taking a risk, I sat down in the empty chair opposite her and hugged my own ribs. Marie, how she had squeezed my arms outside. It was the same thing Anya had done when I fell and she patched me up. I wondered if their grandmother had taught them to show love that way, pressing her finger pads on their bodies to put them back together and then brushing them down.

'However, I am glad you're back. Margaret raised her face to me. 'You look awful, darling.'

'The bruising should be gone in a day or two. It was only a bump, no real damage done.'

She put down the chain and spread her hands flat on the desk. 'Do you want to tell me what happened?'

'I walked into a door. Honestly.'

This was the wrong answer. She was not in the mood for evasions.

'Mairéad, I do not talk about this with every young woman who works for me, but I think you need to hear it before it's too late.' With rapid movements, she took off her glasses, shut her eyes and pinched the bridge of her nose. 'So difficult. Funerals.' When she opened them again, her eyes were clear. 'My best friend died before she was forty. We went to school together, told each other everything. First period, first boyfriend, first time I had a drink was with Sally. What were the chances, do you think, that both of us would become alcoholics? Maybe that's why we were friends. I believe you are struggling with something, Mairéad, and you need to do something about it.'

To hide my discomfort, I picked up the gold chain and began working out the last of the knots. I could hear her inhaling and exhaling.

'You might be expecting me to offer you condolences, but that is not what I'm doing. When Sally died – I am trying not to oversimplify things. When she died, it could have been me. Easily. I said it out loud and someone heard me and the lies stopped for a second. I was sick of being sick. I was scared of getting better. You want it to end, but you also fear it. I think you can understand that. A sudden death can shock you back into life. You've returned to work, Mairéad, and I appreciate it, as I said, but it's all a slightly different colour now, isn't it? The simplest thing seems impossible because you're feeling deeply sorry for yourself and your excuses are endless. Let me advise you, from experience, now is the time to act.'

Feeling sorry for myself? Is that what she thought I was doing? I squeezed the chain between my fingers in order to hold my temper and looked directly at her. She kept on talking.

'Addiction is terrifically boring, don't let anyone tell you otherwise. The same demand, over and over. Isolating you. Ruining your life. It is never happy, never exciting and never enough.' She took her glasses case out of a drawer, snapped it open and started using the square of cloth to wipe her lenses. 'The wanting does not go away. But you can learn to row back from it and keep on rowing back by becoming brutally honest with yourself. And not just when it's easy to do so.'

Her eyes remained clear but there was a quivering in her hands as we both stared at the desk. Margaret and I were not friends. It was possible she didn't like me. I was too much in awe of her to know for sure. If anyone else had presumed to give me a sermon about what was wrong with me, I wouldn't have listened. Except no one else was taking this much trouble to get through to me. Sick of being sick. Afraid of getting better. I released the last knot in the gold chain and stretched the links into a straight line before putting it down.

'Thank you for the card,' I said. 'It meant a lot to me. You are—'

She waved her hand over the telephone to call a halt to my speech. 'I am sorry for blurting it out, about your grandmother.'

'You told me the truth. I'm learning to appreciate that.'

There was a heart-shaped locket next to the phone. Threading it onto the chain, Margaret secured the neck-lace around her throat and tucked it under her blouse.

'Right, let's get on, shall we?' She put her glasses back on. 'Did you get your mobile phone? We had to switch it off, darling. The noise of the thing, you see. I'll need your help this week with shopping for a photoshoot I've been cornered into. Five black jumpsuits, low-cut, red and black heels. They'll be wearing a lot of red lipstick. You can invoice for your hours separately.'

'What's the show?'

'Noël Coward. Oliver is producing *Present Laughter*.

They want the publicity to reference the song 'Addicted to Love'. Five characters in black around Gary Essendine in white. Except one of the five is male.'

'You want me to find a sexy jumpsuit for a man?'

'Cutting-edge stuff, isn't it? We should have measurements for most of them already. Apart from Victoria Holborn. She's new.'

Saturday, 6 April 2002, 11.15 p.m.

'Another birthday?' Philippa said. 'Didn't we just have a birthday? A special occasion is not special if it happens every week.'

'Are you a Puritan now, Philippa?' Jacqui looked pleased with herself. 'What's wrong with celebrating another birthday?'

'I suspect it's made-up. The entire crew seem to have had a birthday during this run. Anyway, it's the mother who should be celebrated, since she did all the work.' Philippa continued to pack her bag.

'You're coming, aren't you, Mairéad?' Jacqui asked. 'It would be nice to have one other person from Wardrobe.'

'Only because it's Lou,' I replied. It was also because I had made it to Saturday and, anyway, birds of a feather. Who else finished work at this time and was asking me to go for a drink with them?

'Enjoy the passive smoking.' Philippa put her arms into her coat and checked the inside pocket for her house keys.

'There will be nothing passive about tonight.' Jacqui went to the full-length mirror and began applying an orange-red lipstick.

'What about the gorgeous Ravi?' Philippa looked confused.

'History.' Jacqui pressed her lips together and then checked her teeth. 'No, actually. Not history, just too many current affairs. Ready, Mairéad?'

'One more pile to sort. Won't be far behind you.'

They left the room together and I decided to push my last two tasks onto Monday's list.

Lou beckoned me over as soon as I entered the bar from the staff corridor. He rested his arm lightly around my shoulders without interrupting the flow of his speech to the small group standing around a circular table with a bottle of champagne in the middle. Jacqui. Alison. Sandra. The other cast members, or the ones who had stayed, had taken seats at a nearby booth. Close enough to hear their laughter, but not what was being said.

'He was deaf, you see, Mairéad,' Lou explained, pressing my arm for a second. 'Said almost nothing, apart from, "Did you come?" No, don't laugh, Sandra, I mean it. I have thought about it a lot since then. Taking the unnecessary ado out of sex. Not just doing it, but really feeling it.' He gave me a friendly kiss on the cheek. 'Take a glass, darling. Socks and jocks all drying on the line, are they?' His attention was obviously on the bar counter. Scott Gilbourne was standing with a different set, his arm around the waist of a petite blonde woman, facing two other couples, talking loudly over one another. After what Alison had said about infatuations, I tried to imagine him scrubbing pots or organising a birthday party. He must have shaved before he came down because he looked brighter than earlier. The white T-shirt made a difference, emphasising his shoulders and chest. So handsome. So disappointing. Whatever speech he would make at his brother's wedding would be set firmly in a world where brides were silently beautiful and grooms were conquering heroes.

I reached around Lou's hips and pulled on his waistband as playfully as I dared.

'Missing one pair of frilly knickers,' I said. 'You wouldn't happen to know their whereabouts, would you?'

Lou threw back his head in delight at the suggestion and bumped his hips lightly against mine: 'Oom-pah-pah!' He returned his attention to the bar. 'See the velvet?' he whispered into my ear.

Beyond Scott and his guests, a figure stood with its back to us, wearing a high-collared velvet jacket that changed from dark green to matte charcoal, like a mallard's neck, as they moved. There was a fine pattern of leaves or feathers embroidered in gold thread down the spine. They had incredible posture, holding a perfect line. Maybe it was because Lou had whispered, or the beauty of the cloth, but I was able to relax the grip in my jaw. I remembered the backs of the pallbearers as they brought the coffin into the church, the icons glowing from the walls.

'Imagine it in candlelight,' I said, 'how it would pick up the gold.'

'Exquisite.' Lou kept his eyes on the velvet while talking again to the group. 'And a silk cravat that would look ridiculous on anyone else. I would remove it very slowly, sliding it out from—' He touched his own breastbone with his fingertips. 'Must be a choreographer. Or maybe a director. This is something I've noticed, especially in portraits: the powerful people keep their throats covered. Why is that?'

'They don't want to lose their head to the guillotine,' Sandra replied.

'I have such a need to fondle the goods.' Lou was transfixed.

'I'd like to meet whoever made that jacket.' I was transfixed.

'Mairéad, you are fucking hopeless.' Jacqui rolled her eyes at me.

A burst of laughter rang out from Scott's group. One of the men had his arms raised over his head as if to catch something and kept checking the empty space between them as the women continued laughing. The man lowered his arms and shook out his wrist to release the gold watch that had slipped over his cuff. Scott passed his hand over his face and hung his head. Whatever the joke, if I had heard it, I would struggle to understand it. It would bother me. I would go to bed agitated about why I had pretended to enjoy it and then I'd be angry that I was the person who did his laundry and no one talked about it.

'Arse,' Sandra said.

There was a slight movement across the back of my neck, as if the wind had changed direction. Lou let go of my arm and I dropped my hand from his waist.

'Here they are, Victoria. Allow me to introduce you to the most talented and attractive company in London.' Only one voice could boom like that. I looked over my shoulder to the main stairwell, where the sound was coming from. Pulling himself up straight as he waited for a young woman to climb the last step. She had such a tiny waist, even Oliver appeared broad next to her. He rolled out his arm in a gallant flourish and they stepped forward. My hips were turning in the opposite direction to my head, one knee bending as I got ready to bolt, calculating the obstacles between me and the staff corridor. As he moved closer, I tried to remain completely still, until I realised he was looking past me. Instead of stopping to introduce his latest star, he put his back to our table, clearing a safe path to the booth where the others were seated.

'Flattery will get you everywhere, darling,' Lou called out. He narrowed his eyes at Oliver's crown, unsmiling. Oliver snapped his head around as Lou made a moue and raised a glass to his employer. I thought it was funny, until Oliver took two or three rapid steps in our direction, stamping one foot flat on the ground as he jutted his chest as far forward as possible, bringing his face aggressively close to Lou's.

'Queers should be seen and not heard.' Oliver's body drew back as he raised his voice. 'Or kept in fucking Wardrobe, where they belong.'

The ferocity was shocking. I had the sensation of trying to escape a nightmare but my limbs were paralysed by sleep. Stupefied. The cash drawer at the bar sprang open and wasn't closed. Customers stared at him. Victoria had dropped her smile and her eyes moved from Oliver to Lou, and back again. She was that woman at the funeral, holding the plate for her husband. I wondered if he had sent Victoria flowers and a first edition, if that had brought her here and if she knew he'd used the same tactics with Alison. The smell of his cologne reached me, like my grandmother's garden at night. My mother could toss that fucker over a crossbar with one arm. My mother, the first to put her head in the lion's mouth, despite what had happened to her. We were doing what Oliver wanted: staying silent. If no one spoke, he would interpret it as agreement and I did not agree. He thought he had finished with us, already returning to his protégée. I pitched my voice squarely at him.

'But then, whose plays would you produce? If you cut out queers, that's most of your repertoire.' Do not cower, I told myself. Do not flinch.

Oliver's face was more frightening than a raised fist. A cold sweat ran from my armpits and I was never so glad to be wearing flat shoes. The coldness I felt was my blood draining inwards, an extreme low tide. His lips curled in disgust and he opened his mouth to speak, but Victoria cut him off with a laugh that could have lifted a sparrow. As he locked eyes with mine, I sensed Lou getting ready to fight and Alison's hand on my arm, and he could not forbid me from showing love for . . . for my . . . from speaking up.

'You're not above a little humour, are you, Oliver?' Alison spoke evenly as she moved closer to my side.

Without breaking his stare, he tilted his head, and I knew it would get worse. Not here, not now, but he was coming back because he wanted me dead. With stomach-turning slowness, he released that awful crocodile smile and held it as he eyeballed each one of us. I wondered how he ever had sex with a willing partner.

'Of course not, darling. He turned to Alison. 'I trust they managed to dress you properly for tonight's performance? I must have a word with Margaret.' Then he twisted away.

Victoria was watching Alison. She parted her lips to say something, then closed them firmly as Alison noticed her.

'Come, Victoria,' Oliver commanded, 'I want you to meet your new confrères.'

The tight smile Victoria held was unsettling. She backed away carefully, as if moving out of the light and upstage.

It was a tiny moment for Oliver, a minor crease, but my heart had slowed to a stop and I needed some sugar if I didn't want to faint. I had gone and made a partridge of myself. There were empty glasses on the table. It didn't matter to me if they were clean or not, I filled one with what was left in the champagne bottle and knocked it back.

'Thank you,' I said to Alison, relieved not to have been bawled out by Oliver in public. I held the table edge to counteract the dizziness.

'I hope he dies alone and in pain,' Alison said.

'He is alone,' Lou said. 'Look at him.'

Oliver was clicking his fingers at the bar staff, signalling for another round for the company. Victoria kept glancing in Alison's direction.

'I was ready to punch the bastard this time. One more drink and I would have.' Lou made a fist with one hand.

'He'd have you up for GBH before midnight, Rocky,' Sandra said, 'and then he'd drag the rest of us into the mess.'

'A deserted Scottish island in winter with nothing but diseased sheep and one leaking boat is where I'd send him,' Jacqui said. 'Victoria Holborn. Cock-burn, more like. Too busy sucking up to say hello to her inferiors.'

'That's what you'll tell her, is it? That she slept with him to get the job. To her face, in the brightest moment of her career, you'll chose that moment to tell her?' Everyone looked at Alison talking into her glass. 'Do you know how many actresses are currently unemployed?' She finished her drink and swallowed. 'Oliver certainly does. At least I won't have to deal with him and his latest crony in my dressingroom, the pair of them watching as I try to get out of the shower.' She raised her eyes to me. 'No one strikes the king and flourishes afterwards. Especially if you confront him when he's entertaining. What on earth made you say it, Mairéad?'

'Death,' I said.

'Ha!' Lou roared laughing. 'Fuck it. Fuck it all! She's right. We're alive, aren't we? And it's my birthday. We're not leaving, we're moving on. To Soho, my loves!' He kissed me on the lips and spun around to speak to the velvet jacket. I could see him smiling as he said, 'Come with us, darlings,' and the beautiful figure and their companions followed him. Scott had turned to prop up the bar as Lou passed by. On purpose, I thought.

We were walking down the stairwell as Mildew Miller was coming up. Guaranteed to be lurking in Oliver's shadow, waiting for another opportunity to garrotte me or crush me against a wall and grope me.

'What's this? Where's the party going, Mairéad?'

'Don't talk to me,' I told him.

He grabbed my wrist and I couldn't shake him off. Jacqui turned around to look at us, came back up the steps to get behind him and rapidly tapped the back of his knees with her foot. He buckled.

'Fuck off, Richard,' Jacqui said and took my hand. She

interlaced her fingers with mine as she broke into a run and took me with her. Oliver's face pursued me as we streamed through the foyer and out of the building. He would get me on my own and make me pay for what I had said. No one would try to stop him and nothing would be done about it afterwards.

'Come on,' I said to Jacqui, letting go in order to raise my arms like a sprinter crossing the finish line. 'Race you to the lights!' I shut my eyes for a second, then opened them wide, banishing Oliver from my mind as I kicked up my heels to go faster.

'Wait until we tell Philippa about tonight,' Jacqui called out, 'especially the part where we started dancing on tables and kissing beautiful men.'

It was so warm. When I stopped running, I wanted to be at home, where I could strip off and jump into the sea. The taste of it was in my mouth. Summer was coming.

Sunday morning, 7 April 2002

They said on the radio that 70,000 people per day were expected at the lying-in-state of the Queen Mother. I was in my own bed, wondering if Jacqui was still out. One minute I had been dancing, the next I was flailing because an older man had grabbed my hips and would not leave me alone. Lou gave me twenty pounds towards the minicab fare. To my rented room and distant house-mates. Samira would be in her bed until this afternoon and Hannah would be with her boyfriend. Get up and do something, I told myself. Make an effort.

Going down to the Tube on my day off was depressing, but I was curious to see it, this slightly different funeral. I made my way to Westminster station and then back up to the daylight.

Lloyd was right about the crowds. 'The place is thronged, Granny Kate,' I whispered, walking against the flow to stand on Lambeth Bridge and watch two miles of people winding around Victoria Gardens, who must have been queuing for hours, patiently waiting their turn. Past my old friend, Oliver Cromwell. A woman opening the clasp on her sturdy handbag caught my attention.

It was the bag and the outfit. Granny Kate called a suit a 'costume'. The heather-pink, the blue tweed, the understated tartan. Her three costumes. With her good handbag and smart shoes. Putting on the costume was what made the occasion special. The woman in the queue took out a hairbrush and combed her bobbed hair, patting it flat at the back. My own hair was tangled from the wind in the underground tunnels. I had no brush with me. Then she checked her blue A-line skirt was centred, seams straight and the tips of the collar on her white shirt were proud of her short jacket. In order to walk past a coffin. I had on an ugly brown fleece and cheap runners. Her dignity brought out the strongest feeling in me. It was a wish, a real desire, to be more like my grandmother. I had not felt it before. In fact, the thought would have annoyed me a week ago. But suddenly I missed her terribly, in this strange city, where nobody knew my home. Granny had tried to fix my hair with two decorative combs once, when I was maybe ten or eleven. Gently and carefully, lifting the strands away from my face and then pushing the combs firmly into position. She had visitors coming. As soon as they sat down together with their tea, I took the combs out, gently and carefully, and handed them back to her.

'She's gone and she's not coming back,' Thomas had said. It didn't help. At all. I wondered if my mother was looking into water and crying quietly, like I was. I could understand why she had been unable to talk, even though I couldn't explain it.

My mobile phone was ringing. I took a tissue from my pocket and dabbed my eyes with it.

'Dervla has changed the locks.'

'Hello, Dad.'

'Did you know she was doing that? I had to stay the night with Thomas, Lord help me. It's like having a duckling follow you around. He's incapable of being alone. I sent him off to visit Kathleen's grave. Let him tell his mammy all about it.'

'What happened?'

'Nothing. Not a thing. Totally out of the blue. Came home yesterday, saw the new locks. She was gone out. Hasn't spoken to me since the funeral. Did she not say anything to you?'

'She's been telling you she's unhappy for years, Dad.'

He raised his voice. 'What do you know about it?'

'Do you think that shouting at me will fix it?' The grabbing hands of the man from last night's dance floor came into my head like a strobe light, pulsing for a second. I elbowed the air behind me to push away the memory and felt the pain in my lower back returning. 'Let her alone,' I said firmly. 'Stop looking for a scapegoat and face up to yourself.'

There was a silence between us. Had I made him uncomfortable? Good. He could delude himself all he wanted, desperate to discover some terrible plot against him. There was no need for me to be a part of it. I couldn't imagine him changing, I could only imagine him getting worse. And what was I going to do? Become more and more self-righteous? It sounded as though he had a radio chat show on in the background.

'What are you listening to?'

'Sports news. Klondike Bay is racing in Sligo at half past three, if you want to put a fiver on her. I'm bringing Thomas, for a day out.' The brightness in his voice when

213

he said this, definitely smiling at the thought of his horse and a trip to the races. 'I can hear traffic there. Where are you?'

I hesitated. 'At Waterloo. Gazing at the dirty old river.'

'In paradise, what! As long as you have the sunset. Tell Julie I won't be long coming over. And she can drop Terry in the drink when I get there.'

'I'll tell her, word for word. Dad?'

'Yes, love?'

'What will you do?'

'I told you, I'm going to the races.' The sigh and the hard swallow that followed were upsetting. He would be completely lost without her.

'Walk tall,' I said.

'Straight in the eye,' he croaked, before clearing his throat. 'When are you coming home?'

I took my time before I answered him, to let myself believe what I was going to say.

'This show will be finished by the summer. I'll come back for a week when it's over.'

'For Bonfire Night? I haven't lit a bonfire in years. Come home in June and we'll make one down at the beach.'

'All right, yeah. I'll bring a bag of marshmallows.'

'Fucking marshmallows? You will not. We'll have proper music and something decent to toast the dead. Marshmallows. The Lord save us.'

I burst out laughing. 'What about a microphone? And an amp. Would you like a massive amplifier and you could sing to everyone across the bay?'

'I would, aye, that'd be more my style. Let Johnny Cash hear me over in America.'

The image of Johnny Cash opening a window at midsummer and hearing my father serenading him made me smile.

'Mairéad, I want you to promise me something.'

'What's that?'

'Don't stay away for too long. Whatever about me and your mother, but that place . . . it doesn't suit people like us. You'll always be a stranger there. That's the truth. Now. I've enough said. I'm going to get on the road for the races. Mind yourself.'

His voice cracked again and he hung up before I could give out to him for sounding like an old man doling out advice after last orders. Thomas would never leave him. I should have told him that. No one loved him more than he did.

A passenger boat moved steadily downriver, exposing the length of the day in its wake. Free to follow my own thoughts. Oliver was a temporary problem. Let him come for me. It was no better to be safe than sorry. I considered visiting all the bridges, as far as the new Millennium Bridge. Or staying put. It felt good, standing still, watching the traffic on the water.

Monday, 8 April 2002

Margaret came into the room at ten past one. I was on a stepladder, hunting through plastic storage boxes on the higher shelves. What I wanted and couldn't find was the right length of brown laces to replace the frayed ones in Sandra Long's Oxfords. The *click-tap* of Margaret's shoes made me turn around. She was wearing a belted coat with a shawl collar and carried a heap of black cloth over her arms. The black took from the lovely dusty pink of her coat.

'Mairéad, I need you to come to my office. Now.'

What had I done? She did not wait for me to respond and I stayed on the ladder until the tapping on the lino stopped, meaning she was inside her office, and gave her another minute to take off her coat. The photoshoot. She had been at the photoshoot this morning. They must have hated the jumpsuits I bought. I had to go to a chain store. Where else would I have found enough of the stupid things?

Her diary was open on the desk and she was transcribing numbers from it onto a notepad as I sat down opposite her.

'Did they hate the jumpsuits?'

'They cut them. Not the seams, the body. Cut them to reveal more skin. Consequently, they are ruined.'

'The hooligans.' I assessed the pile of black material lying on the carpet behind her. Margaret continued writing. A jumpsuit would look ridiculous on me. I couldn't carry it off. People would make fun of my overalls. I took those thoughts and sent them outside. 'Can I have one?'

Margaret ripped the piece of paper away from the pad and held it out for me.

'You will find yourself in the wilderness after today, and these are the people to call when you do.'

Antonia Weld's name and telephone number was at the top of the list she had made. In brackets underneath, she had written: *Former PA, now at the Royal Opera*.

'Do you want me to call Antonia?'

'My parting advice to you is, don't let them put any woman in a tabard or make you work with organza. It is the devil. Make sure you gather up all your belongings and complete your last timesheet before you finish.'

I was deeply confused. 'Whatever it is you want me to do, you'll have to spell it out for me,' I said.

Blood was rising to her face and I thought she was going to throw another folder at me.

'You're fired, Mairéad. You were in the bar on Saturday evening, yes? Well, you got yourself the sack. Oliver ambushed me this morning and I am sorry to say I could not talk him round. It's best to do this part quickly, so we can both get on.'

The rise in her colour was met by a sudden drop in mine.

'Don't, please, Margaret. Don't.' I felt weak. 'He won't see me, I'll make sure he doesn't.'

'It is too late. I did warn you.'

'You can't do this in the middle of the run. It's not fair on Philippa and Jacqui.'

She leaned back a little, away from me, and paused. 'This is not about fairness. We just need to get it over with. May they send you a better producer in your next job.' The redness in her face and her voice was gone. She turned and spoke to the pile of ruined cloth on the floor: 'Take all the jumpsuits, if you like. I certainly don't want them.' Then she turned back to me and closed her diary. 'You need to leave, Mairéad.'

I was not capable of walking across the office to pick up the damaged cloth. My body was in freefall and I had to get out to draw breath. Standing up with my mouth open, I steadied my hands on the doorframe and propelled myself into the corridor from there. As I walked, I felt my collar tightening around my throat and had to take off my T-shirt. My arms stretched away from my sides, struggling against a terrifying riptide. Pulling and grasping for a shoreline that was within two strokes' distance. It would take all my strength to escape from the unstoppable current sweeping me out to sea. When I made it across the threshold, I collapsed to my knees in front of the full-length mirror and put my head on the ground, letting the air touch the bare skin on my back. It didn't take long, a minute, maybe two, until I felt my heart rate become steady and realised the only thing covering my chest was my bra. This made me laugh as I straightened up and saw my reflection.

'We're alive, aren't we?' I said to her, adjusting the underwires to make them sit comfortably before getting dressed again. On my knees, in front of the mirror, I tried to make sense of what had just happened. Cut off, without one word of kindness. What the fuck was I going to do? Go back to what I was at before, everyone sharing one room and eating in public, working on student showcase productions, or – Jesus Christ – devised shows?

I wanted my thoughts to stop racing, I wanted to find a resting point, to loosen the grip of my jaw, stop striving, stop chasing, stop panicking over nothing. I wanted to live my life, not someone else's idea of my life. When my mother had arrived with no warning last autumn, she was running away. I thought about her, at home, deciding what to do about her mother's handmade cardigans, patchwork quilts, Christmas decorations, letters, silverware, death certificate. Stay or go?

'You should come home, if you want to come home,' he had said. His scrubbed fingernails. His beautiful skin. I wanted to hold Iggy's hand.

Margaret's list was on the lino beside me. She had given me the contact numbers of staff in other theatres and a wardrobe mistress. The sky changed every day. I could do this. Leave the St Leonard. Open up and say yes to the next thing. I scanned the room for what was left undone. Writing my own list for Philippa and Jacqui, I added a note asking them to pass on my timesheets to Margaret. There was no way I was stepping inside her office again.

Before I left for good, I went onto the fire escape and stood looking at the people in the opposite building. Taking a notion, I shouted: 'This is my life. Mine. I am the driver!' Then I bowed extravagantly and blew them a kiss goodbye.

'They want me to disappear,' I told Mr Henderson on my way out, 'as if I had never existed. Because of that tyrant. Will you explain what happened to Anya for me? And Lloyd?'

'You keep your chin up, my dear,' he said. 'He'll get his, one day, don't you worry, and I hope I'm there to see it.'

There was nothing else I could think of to tell him. I pitched forwards and backwards on my heels, working up the courage to move.

'I'll miss you,' I said.

'Go on now, there's more to life than this old dungeon.'

On Shaftesbury Avenue, a bus drove past with a T-side advertisement for *La Cenerentola* at the Royal Opera House. From where I stood on the street, I dialled Antonia Weld's number on my mobile phone.

'I've just been fired from the St Leonard,' I said.

There was a light click on the other end, like a lock turning on a door. Antonia took a sharp breath and then released a brief 'Oh!'

'Margaret Gifford gave me . . . Is it all right to call you? I have no . . . I need to find—'

'Welcome to the survivors' group,' she said. 'Where are you now? And can you come to me in Covent Garden?'

'Yes.'

'Go to the box-office entrance. I'll meet you there.'

ACKNOWLEDGEMENTS

This novel began in a *Stinging Fly* workshop. To Sean O'Reilly, Declan Meade and everyone at the Stinging Fly, thank you for nurturing and developing new writers and new writing. For the care and attention given to this story, I am deeply grateful to my agent Eleanor Birne and to the exceptional team at Canongate: to Leah Woodburn for her insightful edits, Jenny Izumi Fry, Jamie Byng, and to the teams in Editorial, Marketing, Publicity, Sales, Design, Rights and Contracts, all of whom hit the ground running, including Amaani Banharally, Rali Chorbadzhiyska, Sasha Cox, Anna Frame, Joanna Lord, Jessica Neale, Gaia Poggiogalli, Vicki Rutherford, Alice Shortland and Charlie Tooke. Thank you also to Gale Winskill for her patient copyedits.

To the costume and theatre professionals who shared their expertise with me, thank you to Kate Beales, Lesley Bond, Derek Conaghy, Ciara Fleming, Donna Geraghty, Sinéad Lawlor, Carol Lingwood, Niamh Lunny, Vicky Miller, Eimer Murphy, Joan O'Clery, Anne O'Leary, Janie Blacksell and to Judith Colthurst at BECTU. Things have changed since 2002, the correct term is now 'Costume Department' and no longer 'Wardrobe'. For your patience with my outdated terminology and inevitable mistakes, I am grateful. The errors in the text are my own.

Sincere acknowledgements are owed to Minister Catherine Martin TD and the Department of Tourism, Culture, Arts, Gaeltacht, Sport and Media in Ireland for the Basic Income for the Arts pilot scheme, of which I am a recipient, and to the Irish Arts Council for an Agility Award in 2021.

Grá mór to my writing group: Sheila Armstrong, Stephen Dineen, Olivia Fitzsimons, Cassia Gaden Gilmartin, Katie McDermott, Louise Nealon and Stephen Walsh. Wholehearted thanks to Danielle McLaughlin for her mentorship and support, to Thomas Morris for his generosity and to Greywood Arts, County Cork, for the space to write an ending. Abiding thanks to Andrew Simonet and Artists U for building a movement, not a brand, and for connecting me with Jules Bradbury, Anna-Lise Marie Hearn, Nell Regan and Vanessa Rolf. Thank you to Siobhán McGuinness for helping me to remember London in 2002, and to Leona Talbot and Nikki Walsh, artists to their core, whose belief in the work never wavered. To the teachers, booksellers, librarians and the staff of our public amenities, this story exists because I was able to spend a lot of time benefitting from the work you do. Táim fíorbhuíoch daoibh go léir.

Thank you to Brendan Barrington for publishing my short stories in *The Dublin Review* and to Kevin Barry and Olivia Smith for including my work in *Winter Papers*.

It is not easy having a fiction writer in the family. The only thing worse than thinking your relative is writing about you is thinking your relative is not writing about you. To my own family, in particular my mother, Peggie Gallagher, my sister-in-law Tracey, my brother John, my nieces and nephews, and my sister, Mary, for her unstoppable strength and for teaching me to climb up kitchen cupboards, a thousand thanks. In memory of my father, Patrick Garvey (1948–2023).

To theatre people everywhere, thank you.

BIBLIOGRAPHY

Chekhov, Anton. *Uncle Vanya*. In: Stephen Mulrine (trans.), *Chekov: Four Plays*. London, Nick Hern Books, 2005.

Heaney, Seamus. *Sweeney Astray*. London, Faber & Faber, 1984, stanza 75, p.77.

O'Keeffe, J.G. (ed.). *Buile Suibhne*. Irish Texts Society Volume 12. First published 1913, reprinted 1996, 2011, stanza 75, p.138.

Woolf, Virginia. 'Mrs Dalloway of Bond Street' and 'An Unwritten Novel'. In: Susan Dick (ed.), *The Complete Shorter Fiction of Virginia Woolf*. London, Hogarth, 1989.